S k i n

a compilation by Pulp Faction

CIP data available from the British Library
ISBN 1-899571-00-0
Printed by Redwood Books

Editor: Elaine Palmer
Associate Editors: Robyn Conway, Darren Bennett
Design: Accident
Art Direction: Bettina Walter & Fabian Monheim
Contributing Designers: Sophia Einarsson, Francis Stebbing
Thanks to Tim Spencer for
Car, Jeep, Fourwheele
Huw Morgan for Garandahand
Francis Stebbing for Lungfat
Cover: Dog Collar by Jenifer Corker

Contents

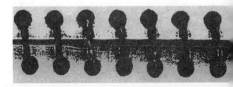

Tattooed Love Letter

Kiran Grewal

Oh YES, life is just hunky dory isn't it, scared stiff of dependence, running around being a lone warrior woman, Ninjette. The space you should have occupied was empty, but somehow you were there with me, at that Transglobal gig in the East End, I go into trance of booming bass and cross-cultural rhythms.

Watching NYPD Blues, unable to engage with the narrative, but recognise a reprimand when I see one, and are police women now recruited from Eileen Ford's model agency? Charlie's Angels in vogue again, LIPGLOSS.

'Hey now, Hey now, what's the matter with you, you know girls just wanna have fun, that's all it is,' sing Cyndi Lauper and Clive, the would-be teenage gangster. We talk philosophy and art while his peers throw bricks at passers by. 'Bad boys in a England, Rude boys in a London', sings General Levy as we hurtle back to the remand centre for Rice Crispies and a game of pool, BOOYAKA, says Clive.

Are you on drugs, your eyes are glazed'. It's hardly surprising, this place and everyone in it is full of nothingness. False community, play my role, but I'm shutting off, I cannot relate to you, your vulnerability renders me guilty, and I cannot take you home or look after you. But it's not my fault, no one is home, the walls are thick like a fortress, the boundaries are invisible, cross the line and feel the deterrent, you'll feel your body and soul freeze, faintly perceptible convulsions of electric shock stun you into a state of limbo.

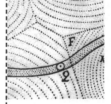 He has a preoccupation with sex and his looks, tall, graceful but so aggressive, it intrigues me. I'm reminded of my first love, and you. 'I'll love you forever, if you lend me 50p'. He leans close, I can feel his breath on my face, his lips brush against my hair. I try not to touch him when I hand him the cigarette. He reminds me of once how I felt oh so in control and so immortal, my head full of odes to that obscure object of desire, knowing I would soon be swooning in the arms of the mythical man beast, who would rescue me from a fate worse than death; conventional coupledom and a semi-detached home just for two, forever and ever.

I used to lie awake at night petrified by the thought of commitment, yet wanting a fairy-tale, glorious technicolour romance, but the mythical man beast made me unhappy with his demands and questionable superiority, and a seemingly complete lack of heroic deeds.

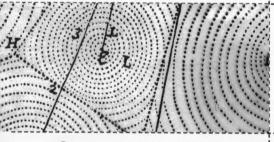

Already toying with the games of domination and submission, learning the rules as you walk away from your safe suburban home at dawn, you are hoping to discover excitement and adventure in Paris or Amsterdam.

So London is calling again, burni again, the shop windows a smashed, I saw it on tv, the battle of Pa Lane, you were there, moving with t crowd. I hoped you'd be ok, and not g hurt or arrested, or fall in the path of monumental police horse.

Walk around London Town, hardly aware of people, they are looking for happiness through the purchasing of consumer goods. I squirt myself with a perfume named 'SUCCESS', which smells of champagne and boiled sweets. This is comforting but the feeling is still hollow, success is a dream that you can now buy in a bottle, will it transform my life?

Run, Run, Running away from the h ow intimacy of a stranger's eye smiling eyes boring into my soul, but only a physical reaction. I'm scared, scared that there is nothing more th mere lust, just like before.

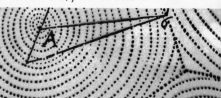

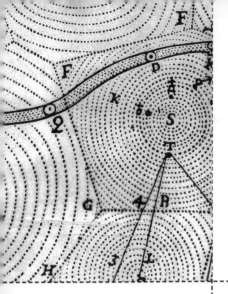

There was for a moment no concrete past and the future was an open book, moving quickly and purposefully, the camera filming my footsteps, and moving to the rhythm of my walk.

t's ALLRIGHT, It's ok, chanting to myself, where are you when I need ›u? Envelope me, hug me, I want to lose yself in you. Your hands are like a sculp->rs hands, bigger than mine, I could ever bear to be touched by soft pale ands which are smaller than mine. I want › lose myself in you, ok, so it doesn't ways seem that way. I'm preoccupied ith thoughts of survival, being able to ay the rent and still achieve some of my reams.

There is a hurricane over the Gulf of Mexico, and you are living with Stig f the dump, who tells me he wants to ake money.

Flying over the oceans, immersed in the clouds, I left my life behind, 'Oh s gonna be a bright, bright, bright, sun- niney day,' walking down Market Street, rrounded by the gentle animal roar of e traffic. I was FREE.

So far away from the reality of a hum- drum, routine filled existence in the city which offered very little surprises, I was floating like in a dreamscape. Climbing the hills, and looking down at the bay of San Francisco, sharp intake of breath.

The pale grey skyscrapers and the Pyramid Building were barely visible in the distance, enveloped in a soft focus bog. From the balcony of the institute of Fine Art, I gazed at this city, this feeling which made my heart beat faster, in court- yard of the temple of learning I made enquiries about how to enrol.

8

SOARING from this freedom, and light-headedness, I went down to the Haight and got myself a small blue and purple butterfly tattoo on my shoulder.

You seemed so far away, as you were, but even on the telephone your voice was distant and barely seemed to know me, although you had moved into my flat. Angry and confused I went to find myself in the city again, speeding up and down hills at night, Sutter and Davisdero, down to the nightclub in the company of two deadhead yuppy girls I vaguely knew, who I observed with curiosity as they showed me the bright lights of the city.

The ex-London girl drove like a maniac, wildly putting her foot down on the accelerator. The doorman was a Mancunian Sisters of Mercy reject. Inside, the familiar London music caused a glow of recognition.
'Laiadi, Laladay, She's homeless, oh she's homeless, Laiadi, Laladay'. Someone asked me to dance, I was transported to School Village Hall discos, he asked if I was Italian and I shook my head, trying to catch the eye of a guy who really interested me, maybe because he looked a bit like you.

Back in London, I was shocked to se how dirty and dusty and sad the fl looked. You stood by the radiator, yo blond hair drooping. I immediately starte to clean up, in an attempt to transfor the environment and situation, then showed you my butterfly tattoo and filme you on video, all smiles and kitchen ute sils, you said you wanted a tattoo too.

arlier, on a bed somewhere, I imagined our bodies
gether, our boundaries dissolving until we became one, one unit, a puddle
are deliquescing. Like an x rated special effect,
of organic matter on the floor.
we were melting

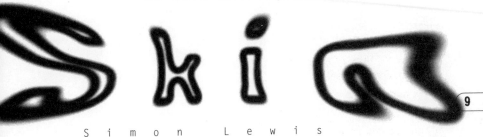

Simon   Lewis

he dug at my flesh with her finger. 'Mine, mine,' she said, pulling

and tearing at the skin of my chest, as if trying to break in.

This dream. My body is hollow. There is nothing inside but air.

am punctured and *pffw!* I deflate, like a balloon, and lie on the

floor until she picks me up and puts me in her collection.

When we finished things went weird for me for a while, the world

ooked pale and at an angle. I spent the best part of a day in the

bathroom, shaving off all my hair. I started with my legs and

orked up. The sink soon became clogged. My whole body felt like a

mass of nerve endings. I was raw and innocent, pure again.

ater, on a beach somewhere, I looked at all the lazy people around

e. All that frank anatomy. I wanted everyone to have a Barbie Doll

crotch. I wanted everyone to be smooth and hairless with

perfect skin like plastic.

Skias

A bit

Barry Adamson

Under the Weather

The eight day depression snuck up on Casey's whole being like a change of season. Although there had been a time of splendour that moved him between carnival winds; it was indeed the pinnacle of summer, blazing in its wondrous composition. A shiver, autumnal in its presence, let him know that he had bought it all and was now being hood-winked to the gills and the nights began drawing in all on a solemn moment of thought that gave way to the absolute truth that the vacation was over baby and Casey was off the playlist.

The moon spat down on Casey.
'Fuck you and lovers in Love.'
It grinned its silvery grin, more powerful than anything Casey could invent in this solitary moment. 'If it's an eight day depression,' Casey mused to himself, 'then is this day one or two?' Come to think of it, when that stupid

dog looked at our Case the other day and he'd
asked it to surprise him and say something he
could understand, just any fucking thing, take
him in his confidence and tell him: 'Okay Case,
you're dead right. We've been talking shit for
centuries man and you bought the whole bark.' No
such luck and Casey, well that just got him mad-
der than a pocketful of irony and so one could
be right in assuming that when he went to pet
the mongrel and carefully took a front paw in
each hand and SNAP as he quickly yanked them
apart, the poor little thing's heart pooping in
two as its beautiful brown eyes looked deep into
Casey's and then the mutt spluttering: 'Thanks
man, I thought you were with me,' before flop-
ping in a heap on the ground, that Casey was
already well into it... and that was already
five days ago...

Garth Brooks, everything sucks... Casey smiled
at the ease with which shit that fell on the
wrong side of the tracks leapt into his mind-
frame when he was at this place. Where did it
all come from? and why now did everything look,
smell, taste, feel and sound... like chewing gum
that had been in his mouth for ever? 'If I could
fix my mind on one positive thing, I could cut
this fucker short,' he thought. After all, the
notion of an eight day depression was founded
only on the fact that somebody had told him once
that they were stuck in an 'eight day' and by
day six, when it was just getting good, they
were able to glimpse a positive, which opened
the door to orderly thought and stopped it
short. It was like the idea that you could drink
a zillion cups of coffee and sure enough the day
would arrive when some joker mentioned about doing
the same thing and not being able to sleep and then...
what do you know? So... this in no way was going to

work for Casey because he knew that the power of suggestion could be looked at both ways. And judging by the way that dog had looked at him, orderly thought was the last thing he would now be capable of and what lay ahead was probably nothing short of a personal hell in which he would have his insides out and they were going to stay out because Casey had bought the whole fuck-ing deal and now it was time to collect.

Casey got up and walked to the window. His left leg was dead and he wasn't sure if this was first in a series as he hobbled to the sill.

A stone hit the window at a terrific force, shattering the glass and sending a slice across Casey's face and opening up a wound that poured forth a darker colour than he recognised from the time he was ten and that kid from around the way had tried to steal his 'Wagon Wheel' and Casey had pushed him into touch, the kid hitting his head on a rock and bleeding too much, Casey noticing its thickening qualities but... this was something else.

Just before Case dipped from the window, he noticed a small boy wearing a dog collar which, at the time of the glass connecting with his face, he thought to be rather odd.

He started to feel dizzy, and sat down again. There wasn't even a mirror in the place and so Casey didn't know how bad the cut was, although... that much blood? That really was a bit of a worry. His hands became shaky and an image, too

quick for him to gauge, flashed across his
mind. He coughed... and felt the urge to throw
up and cry all at the same time.
The eight day depression had been counteracted
by something far more troublesome; the murky,
angry, shameful truths that lay underneath its
flimsy coating. Another flash, a woman, more
blood...? No, surely no. He breathed a sigh of
relief when he saw the blood on his hands and
remembered his open wound dilemma. He stood up
quickly to get some tissue, or something that
he could start to mop up the mess with. It was
as though a lightning bolt had struck him
directly through the top of his head and, the
next thing he knew, he was flat on the floor
minus one eye which had been struck out as he
caught the corner of the table on his way
down. The force of the 'lightning' had helped
him to miss out on what he thought would be a
painful experience.

**Casey thought about the dog to clear his mind a little but
every time he did, he saw only its snapping jaws around his
neck, so he thought he'd better give that a miss. There
seemed to be blood everywhere now and Casey's impaired
vision didn't help either.** His stomach lay in his throat as
the flashes, intercut with the dog yapping and snapping, became
clearer. 'Oh my God,' whispered Casey as her face, fixed in an
empathetic gaze but with her heart cut out of her chest, mingled
with other images from years of it.
In his horror, Casey rubbed his face as one truth, brutal in its
revelation, was superceded by another. The image would not leave
him as she opened her eyes and gave him a look that said: 'Why,
Casey. Lovers in Love is such a beautiful melody and its swirling
key change brings a tear to my eye.' Without even realising it,
Casey had opened his wound much more than he could guess. The
image of a dead sweetheart could always guarantee a disconnection
with the cogs of reality. He tried to scream out her name; maybe
even get a chance to explain but nothing short of nothing would

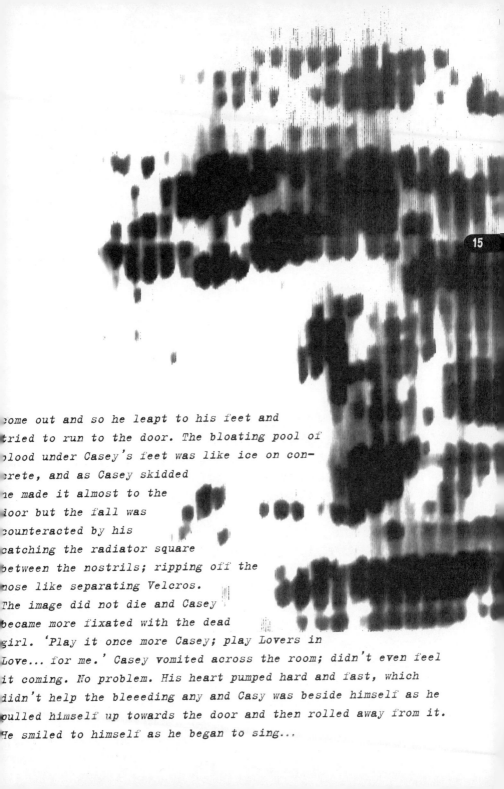

come out and so he leapt to his feet and
tried to run to the door. The bloating pool of
blood under Casey's feet was like ice on concrete, and as Casey skidded
he made it almost to the
door but the fall was
counteracted by his
catching the radiator square
between the nostrils; ripping off the
nose like separating Velcros.
The image did not die and Casey
became more fixated with the dead
girl. 'Play it once more Casey; play Lovers in
Love... for me.' Casey vomited across the room; didn't even feel
it coming. No problem. His heart pumped hard and fast, which
didn't help the bleeeding any and Casy was beside himself as he
pulled himself up towards the door and then rolled away from it.
He smiled to himself as he began to sing...

My body aches for your tenderness once more
My arms dangle around quite useless
These swollen hours of quiet don't help me at all
This heart I have now built a fortress
Until life has a meaning that won't
fail to surface
And the storm gives way
Lovers in Love is what we'll be
And what we'll stay...

The door flew open and two uniformed men pulled their gun
simultaneously and blew Casey's brains clean out of his head
'Thank fuck that's over. Why don't you call the girl'
parents and tell them the bastard's done with...' 'Right yo
are. I wonder what happened here?' 'He looks a bit under th
weather if you ask me.' The two men then took turns kickin
Casey in the balls until the Ambulance came
'Lovers in Love indeed.

Strange Toes

Jacqeline Lucas Palmer

And I might have said would you
Made off down the road all awkward and shy
Do we suddenly hold hands
Since I asked do I kiss you
And what if your breath tasted sour
Smell undesirable and we're stuck in my room
Surely not coffee and strained conversation
A last ditch attempt to convince me I know you
My two seater couch would I pull you towards me
Use the stuff turned my lover to melt in my hands
And you sit undissolved
Speak loud unaffected
And my previous hot panties cool slowly but sure
As I lay you beside me on my celibate throne
Unmoved by the honour you lay there unknowing
I take you the best way and you think you got lucky
Stick my head in the intimacy of your thigh
And it lies there all strange even small and soft maybe
And we wish we were sleeping as I take you inside me
And assume little outbursts of pleasure
And we've dealt with the durex with deft little giggles
The tissues the toilet do we toss and turn sleepless
Do I listen for snoring
May I lock toes with yours?
Do you tell me you're off now with your spunk on my belly
Am I lucky my fingers never circled your nipples
My tongue never followed the nape of your neck
When I saw you
The next time
Our toes might remember.

3 Times

Helen Tookey

1. THC

At first there is laughter, breathless waves of hysteria. But the waves sweep in unidentifiable time, a second or a minute like a stretched bubble forming and unforming, a flow or a frame seeking the next frame but only changing its own edges, I cannot hold it down, it could be a second or an hour.

So there is a jerk out of the waves of laughing because I have the fear of not recognising the speed of time any more, I could have been laughing for days and I must open my eyes to see what has changed, I think everyone has watched me for hours.

No-one watches me   I concentrate and see it has been seconds or minutes only, the same track plays although I thought there had been many others.

I fall back into the desperate sea and I claw out of it again, fall and then claw

The laughter sinks away a little and I concentrate, I grip firmly, I fix my eyes. I try to be sure of the speed of time but it must be slower than my thought because I know, I have seen, have heard, what will come next, what someone will say, I wait some heavy fraction of time for it to happen but it does not, and I am surprised but at once I know what is to come after, but it does not

and these waves are faster than pulse than breath than movements of the eye   faster than frames through the shutter   a dizzy terrible speed a continuous flicker of knowing and not knowing, knowing and surprise, knowing and disorientation, orient and disorient into nausea and inexpressible unnoticed fear

Something is said and it falls into this bending time   it flickers so fast and I thought I took an hour to turn my eyes It was said into distortion It was at once anticipated with clarity and slowed to meaninglessness at the furthest reach of memory Was it I who said that   when was it said it fell into a bending swooping wave   I cannot locate it at any point on any line   I cannot clearly isolate this I

2. LSD

A blue sky and the sun edges the clouds with gold and it looks huge and beautiful. Limitless skies of changing colours. Skies   the infinite heat

f the sun   clear endless space absolute
old   silence passing breath, life
   The clear sky recalls those beautiful
mpty reaches
   The calm drift
   beyond the pull of the tides
   the stirrings of the air
   the sea swell
   beyond the circle of colours
Come now, and I will tell you the only ways
f enquiry that are to be thought of'
   Beyond troubling divisions and
   distinctions
   the world waxes and wanes as a whole
   the most beautiful eternal endless void
   here the truth that could not be said,
   shows itself
   absolute identity
   'It is all one to me where I begin, for
ere again and again I shall return'
hole and of a single kind and unshaken
nd perfect
   an infinite expansion
e calm drift

MDMA have stepped
nto this space
in high boots
is firmly bounded on every side, but it is
igger inside than out
his is another secret space of colour,
movement and sound

but this is the first space with other people
in it
a multiple secret   a space of dance
nothing else is possible
'you are going to dance, and your feet will be
like white doves, like white flowers that
dance upon the trees'
higher than the sun
   I have never really danced before
there is a girl in silver
she looks so happy   I smile at her
and she kisses me
there is a boy dancing
I am so hot
he blows cool breath onto my closed eyes
my only desire is to give you exactly what
you want in the instant you become aware
of wanting, so that I can see your smile
your only desire is water and ice and my
smile
   I have never really danced with you
before
you are a silhouette with haloes and stars
you are transfigured in light and sound
the air between us is in flames
your eyes   your fingers trail jewels
my diamonds burn
   outside this is debated and deathly
but I have never known a world this close
this vision could kill me
but nothing else is possible
I could find no other way to love you so
completely in an instant

3 ... Spaces

3x

19

Joe Ambrose

Tales

That was the 70s. Like they say, that was then and this is now. I was living in Rathmines, a Dublin flatland suburb right alongside the city centre. Sleazy then. Students and petty criminals and guys in bands. The only all-night shop was dark and treacherous, owned by this wild Provo guy who looked like one of the Moors Murderers. The shop was called The Honey Pot. One night I saw a guy pissing into the sliced pans. But you could get tomorrow's papers there, and tea and milk and wine. I'd meet guys from bands there, and the actor Gabriel Byrne would go there a lot to buy papers and cigarettes. He's a big star now, but then he was just a guy. Big tall guy with a taller blonde girlfriend, She was an intelligent television presenter. I was just a guy then too, and Dublin was just an insignificant, backwater, interesting city.

I spent the night in the flat of my comrade, Jamie, the snakeboy. he made his money from miscellaneous criminal activities. A criminal indeed but no thug. Jamie came from upmarket South Dublin seed mixed with respectable country people. His family home bordered onto the home of one of Ireland's Presidents, who was a senior Government Minister when he lived there. Jamie said he was a regular asshole. His mother confirmed this, mentioning the fact that she had voted twice for him when he ran for the Presidency, knowing that he would have to vacate his home. She bought it when it went up for auction so there would be no more neighbour problems. Jamie and me used to kind of squat there sometimes.

Jamie was a criminal by choice, not from necessity. The best kind of criminal. The cool intelligent type, and he lived like a young king. King in exile. King of the wild frontier. Political guerrilla leader in the war against the bourgeoisie.

Maintained a three-roomed flat with hookahs and machetes and guns and snakes and lizards. He was fascinated by explosives and by snakes. He had a lethal small black swamp snake, and a couple of congenial pythons.

There was a very rare, sad, lizard.

He was 16 then and I was 23. On the night in question we'd spent several hours discussing queer bashing. He'd been in a queer bashing gang when he was younger. Jamie was 14. He'd go with his dudes to Palmerston Park, where all the Dublin boy-hookers worked then. Jamie would lean against a well lit tree, the rest of them would hide in the bushes. Jamie would wait for the queer and the queer never took long because Jamie always looked pretty good. He'd walk, hand in hand with the queer, to some nearby dark and obscure spot. There they'd kick the shit out of the victim and rob him. Jamie was disengaging from that kind of life when I met him. He was wrestling with the more adult aspects of entertainment.

All that night, a Saturday night, we listened to reggae music and snorted cocaine and looked at books and comics and magazines. And it was kind o Beckett-like too, like it often is wi cocaine. By 9 in the morning he wa wiped out and it was time to g

As I got up to go he gave m a present of this book, th Amphetamine Manifest a look at the drug scen from the inside.

Outside in the real world it was bright sunny Sunday morning. ambled down Leinster Road with view to walking through Rathmin to my own place for sleep. I lived about half a mile from Jamie. I made lots of money too. I was prosperous in the 70s. Had all the hip records.

I was born a Catholic like most people, and like most people it was –then at least– a Once A Catholic Always A Catholic thing. So when I found myself in front of the b grim Rathmines Catholic Churc I couldn't pass without having look inside. There was a Pop Mass or Fo Mass or whatever the fuck they used to ca them taking place.

The priest was doing his sermon. It was 'Youth Mass' so most of those presen were young Catholics. There was also, course, the occasional pervert in attendanc

22

Mainly it was fat boys and skinny girls. Lots of acne problems in evidence. Dykey females and faggy males.

Drugs and sex is a known combination, but sex and religion is an equally interesting combination. The priest was in his early 40s, covered in a layer of eunuch-like fat. He had a real repressed fag voice. Prim and proper and frustrated and virginal. Some priests I like. Older priests. These new priests grew up as fat provincial closet cases, and they lead seedy lives in the city, victims of their own cowardice and dishonesty. The morning I saw this guy, he was going on at length about fucking around. He had a lot to say about it, and he knew he was getting to the correct target audience. There wasn't as much fucking around in the 70s as people let on, but it was certainly possible. A piggy girl eyed me up and I was about to throw up so I fled the Church. I puked in the courtyard while, inside, they were singing Michael Rowed The Boat Ashore.

I walked up the main street towards my own flat. Old newspapers and cigarette boxes and used condoms and beer cans littered the pavement. I stopped off at the corner shop to buy Sunday papers and some milk. Walked up to my house, a tall impressive redbrick. A flat a floor. I had the second floor. Underneath me lived this guy in his late 30s. He had his window open and I could see him talking to somebody inside. He was playing a Frank Sinatra record.

I looked up at my own place. 'That's my place,' I said to myself. 'I live there. I got all my clothes and my address book and my stuff there. It's the place for my stuff. What the fuck will I do with all this shit?'

Soon it would be my birthday. I took the keys out of my pocket and opened the front door. In the hall there was a note from a girl who'd come around for a fuck. It went: 'Hi. I brought around some Pot Noodles and some beers. Call me if you get in later.' I threw the note in a rubbish bin and went upstairs.

Inside my own flat it was cool and peaceful. I put on a New York Dolls album, walked into the bedroom, slumped onto the bed and fell asleep.

ViRGiN

PReNaTaL SCAN ShOW

SCReAm

Her fierce stride and her spear held high didn't open out her route. The tourists fumbled against her. They fumbled against each other Slow start stop. She danced around their slow start stop and all her intent followed the straight speeding line of her spear. That kind of dance in the direction of Angus.Not the kind of dance when, at the airport, after the memory of his separate parts, his ears and elbows, his teeth and feet had come together in one body. When she was released from the gangway tunnels into corridors feeding passengers into the Welcome Lounge. She danced because she was seeing him. He was there. And she danced forward until she stopped at his frown and his teeth, upper and lower locked against her. And she locked to slow but keep walking. She walked until at his sock up his trouser, his shirt to his throat and all the way up she identified he was dyed the same bile acid green. His all purpose teeth and dimples had switched to on and locked into capital letters. She hadn't remembered the colour of his eyes and of course they were green. And his hair, still his hair but lit from behind by fluorescent tube, a bitter greenish perennial border.

And then he'd spoken. He'd opened his teeth to her. And in small acidic pronunciations shreds of words in one colour, not catching in his teeth like spinach, he'd spat out each one, each undiluted and perfectly formed letter and they'd stuck on her and stained.

Outside the air conditioned, fluorescent day or night, winter or summer, in the heat of the midday sun, his colour had drained. The plug pulled out The plughole vortex. She'd dreamed, at the top of the green, she'd cut off his head. Cut through his neck at his throat

MaRy :

CReAm iNside ECToPic EGg

get to the words and she'd sunk down his plughole vortex and there was only air and
ood behind his words. He'd cut off her words and he'd found in her, he thought,
oughts that were suspiciously not the same as his own. And now the paving stone slabs
ere continuing by themselves to a fruit-box.

'You can't hide anything from me!'

The crowd opened in front of Angela and crowded back against each other. On his fruit-
ox, under the overhead railway, on top of her straight line to the bus stop, he whipped the
rd of his microphone. He spat across the paving stones, against the backs of retreating
gs shoulders and necks. The bus stop was the terminus for the 22, the 17 and the 134.
ne 134 was direct to Angus' door and there was the 134. The doors were shut. The driver
ad a magazine. She cut across the aim of the microphone.

'YOU.' his finger speared at her. 'YOU cannot hide ANYTHING from ME! I – am FULL
F JESUS CHRIST and YOU are FULL of the DEVIL!' he spat. It stuck in his beard.

'That fat gut isn't full of Jesus Christ,' Angela thought. Angela was speaking at the same
me. The crowd were curious, a participating audience. The bus driver behind his door
ad his magazine.

'The driver might let me on so I can shut the fat gut out,' she thought or did she say?
Above the front door where the number had been – where had the numbers been? There
ere letters above the door and the letters spelled B-A-D.

'If I tell the driver what happened and he lets me on and he shuts me into the bus with
m and this is some kind of conspiracy with that fat gut and I'm being paranoid...'

The exhausting whiter than white T-shirt abloat with Jesus burst a blow from his beard
gainst her.

'You're on your way to HELL!' He stabbed at her. The doors swung open to her.

Onto the bottom step, pain shrieked her to her knees. The driver stood from his driver's
eat. He dropped his magazine. Dropped open and facing Angela to
ad 'The Virgin Mary Has No Body.' And as she read her eyes prickled
ack stars and her bones folded back on the paving stones.

the Mother of Jesus and it's just as well he wasn't home because she didn't have anywhere to stay and I was her only friend she said and she hadn't slept for five nights and the next time she rang she was ringing from the secure unit and she said I couldn't have been on the other end of the phone because I was with her...'

'Someone call an ambulance.' A whirlpool of tourists blessing faces.

'Don't move her. There's blood. She's injured her back.'

A face in shadow fish eyed over Angela. A golden halo in front of the sun.

'Put out your tongue,' said the woman. 'It's Rescue Remedy. Star of Bethlehem for 'trauma' and numbness, Rockrose for terror and panic, Impatiens for irritability and tension, Cherry Plum for fear of losing control and Clematis for passing out.'

'Thanks, you're right.' Angela said. She thought 'Like a baby bird opening wide for the worm. That whole nest of them, sitting round the table, tongues quivering, 4 drops each for extreme cases that need rescuing. And her. SHE wasn't there because she was too late to be rescued.'

The first corolla of faces staring from extended vertebrae tucked back down into their necks while the second corolla fitted over the shoulders of the first.

'An ambulance is on its way.'

'I can't...I'm going to...' Angela spoke with an alien tongue. She heard their words. She heard her own words.

'Have some wine Angela. The party's started. We didn't want to start without you.'

'Where's the party?' Angela thought she heard her words.

'At your place. It's your party and it's our surpris party,' said Alison, Trish, Patrick and Sean.

'I locked all the doors.' said Angela.

'We have your spare key,' said Alison, Trish Patrick and Sean.

'I don't have a spare key.'

'Will everyone please move back. We have to get this lady onto a stretcher,' said the ma in uniform doing his job.

'I can't go to hospital,' said Angela.

'You HAVE to go to hospital.' He'd heard her. 'It's the law. It's a citizen's obligation to call an ambulance if someone collapses in a public place. Hey! Her back. Careful how you move her. The hospital will decide whether o when you're fit to leave.'

The spearing siren, the lights, the body raised on a mobile stage. Through the cinem and theatre queues and the traffic. The dramatic highlights. The oxygen mask, the drip, the life and death high speed chase, the exiled heroine. A thought provoking, mature performance. An immaculate production.

A new generation ambulance without the

3

discretion of frosted glass. A white hearse. Celebrity status through the crowded streets. In black it might be spelled out as a floral epitaph. DAD or GRANDMA or the embarrassing pet name naked in one word. The last joke's on you PUFFY.

'Am I destined to be a one word floral tribute?' asked Angela.

'You're nearly there,' spoke another man in another uniform. The ambulance squealed on two wheels. The stretcher tilted but Angela was strapped on securely.

In the corridor, on the trolley, she was strapped on securely. A row of stone usted saints, ecstatic against the length of the wall, their plight highlighted by fluorescent tubes. Along the corridor, Angela was queue jumped past more bodies strapped onto trolleys, straight cketed against escape. Was this a mind, body or spirit hospital? Angela had read about the high suicide rate in places like his. The place where you wait, anxiety at reaking point. The hours of waiting for a diagnosis. Admissable or inadmissable. Pass or fail or certifiable. The most enduring survivors, those with the Munchausen syndrome, if inadmissable,

then to go home and do their own surgery in their own kitchens and bathrooms. She'd read too how they'd clogged up the casualty queues along with the Saturday night car crashes and overdoses.

'An overdose? What did she take?' the starched nurse was asking.

'If I remember rightly, it was 15 Rohypnol, 10 Mogadon, 12 Valium – 50 milligrams.'

'You saw the bottles?' The nurse recorded the details.

'She always wrote it all down. What she took. How many she could take before...' That was Sean's face. Sean's face in the crowd at the bus stop. This was Sean's face at the hospital....

'For Christsake get her stomach pumped,' he heightened his whisper.

'Can I see a doctor? Will a doctor please give me a diagnosis!' shouted Angela.

'What's she saying?' said the nurse who wasn't taking notes. She hailed a porter. 'I can see what's wrong with her. Get her a sedative!'

'You and your auras,' said the note taking nurse, both of them aerosol blonde above the starch.

'I'd save them a fortune in time and funding. If these cases were just sent to me there'd be no need for wasteful X-Rays, dissection – exploratory – it's a scandalous waste and it's more than time I lodged a formal complaint.'

'What's wrong with me then?' shouted Angela.

The note taking nurse clenched.

'Will you – please – keep your voice down. Apart – from a rather sluggish colon... Have you tried irrigation? No? Whatever the toxicity that's working out through your emotional body, it's originated from a long and festering period of unexpressed hostility...'

'Yes yes. I know,' said Angela.

'....polluting your psyche with a murderous rage. You could well, therefore, contaminate the corridor. There are so many vulnerable bodies around and that would be selfish. We can't risk a plague on our hands. Can we? So, therefore, we can't keep you here any longer.

'Can I leave then?'

'I beg your pardon. We have a responsibility to the public. More specifically, that innocent member of the public, even now, who awaits unwittingly to suffer the festering consequence of your festering primal condition. I am an advocate of preventative medicine. Forgive. Always remember. Forgive. There's nothing yet to cut out of you. But we allow your condition develop any further, we will, almost certainly, have to. Your condition will solidify. You'll be full of lumps the size and weight of...'

She turned to the witnessing nurse – 'those fossilised dinosaur eggs. You know the ones I mean? On telly the other night. What night was it?'

'Tuesday. Weren't they amazing! When they opened them up the babies were still inside.

'Excuse me. Excuse me. Is anybody there?' shouted Angela. 'I am extremely angry and was extremely angry and I have an extremely good reason to be extremely angry.'

'Quieten down! Please! If your solar plexus area was leaning more towards magenta, I'd say fine. Who am I to stand in your way? But no. You can't deceive me, even if you're willing to deceive yourself. Your solar plexus area – the spleen, bile and gall – they're a curdle of fermenting scarlet...'

The porter returned. He leaned the underside of his jaw and his loose adam's apple over Angela's face.

'We're out of Valium. I'm sure this Cocktail will suffice.' he said.

'That's very nice. Thank you Nurse. Now then my lady...Where are your veins? You're hiding your veins. Where are they? In such a blatantly physical matter my visionary gift isn't always relevant. Nurse, will you – please...'

The porter hauled his shirt out from his trousers. Leaning over Angela's face, he tourniqueted tight above her elbow. To him, her vein was blatant and he syringed the cocktail in. The blood of Angela foamed in the syringe.

'Blood. Oh. Such a dreadful scarlet,' staggered the nurse. 'Take her to the priest!'

Angela was travelling backwards. Against each set of swing doors her head was a battering ram. Two fried eggs sliding on fat. Two bowls of gelled caviar. Her eyes multiplied the lightbulbs. Fly eyes. A fly's point of view. Her probiscus tongue unravelled towards the source of light. A long, thin string that flopped again into the shout shape of her mouth. Her jaw locked open, unlocked and snapped shut. Her jaw rotated, pushed and ground. The Venus fly trap and the fly were eating each other. Each set of swing doors ground her tongue between her jaws.

'Her treatment can start with a confession. He won't give her absolution tonight. Perhaps you could jump the queue. In her condition.'

She couldn't see the face of the porter nurse. She remembered the underside. Checking left, checking right. At the intersections, he was a defensive driver. Left or right, his mouth spread below his ear. His ear dawdled on top of his nose, his nose on top of his ear. His eyes, a string of beads around his head and each bead fringed in short, pale hairs. Did a veil of pale hair grow from his face? Did he walk backwards or was he walking sideways as well as forwards?

No reassuring small talk to the anaesthetised, the drunk or the dead. Bodies were the same and they were pushed along the same corridors. He pushed her head into a door that didn't open. He pushed harder. She was trying to tighten her eyes to focus. The doors opened into a lift. He leaned across to pull the last of her in. A white nylon canopy shut out the lights. She sniffed. Somewhere up there beyond the nylon there was an arm pit. The doors closed.

Down

Down

Under the earth the doors opened into a tunnel of low, long pipes and ducts. A traffic light green changed to amber then red. Naked light bulbs rolled to a fidgeting rhythm. Through the wall, a wall thickened by ancient dirt, a train drew parallel. The train passed. The doors of the lift opened. A mountain of linen on a trolley soared towards the porter. He backed to the wall. A soft pressure of linen stink, a soaring mountain of blotted body fluid, blotted out the underarms as Angela inhaled its length from her feet to her face. The light turned to green. The mountain passed. The

porter pushed on. The mountain of stink
finished at a door in the wall. The wall
with the train on the other side.

The doors of the lift shook open again.

The porter stopped. The porter waited.

'How's it going mate?'

'How's it going mate?'

The other porter pushed another trolley
and another body. He stopped by another
door on the other wall. A plain label in
plain lettering. MORGUE.

'Busy?' said the porter of Angela.

'Another Saturday night. You'd better
cover her up before you take her in. That
sheet back there. Off the laundry. Pissed
on. Not that she'd notice.'

'She's not dead yet.'

'Whatta you doing with her down here then?'

'Short cut to the priest.'

'Last rites or what? Oh look, she's
looking at me. What's her name? What's
your name?'

'She's out of it. No ID. No IQ. You
should've heard her. I bet they're glad to
be rid of her.'

'What's she in for?'

'Something malignant.' Tap, tap on his
forehead. 'Specially up here.'

'No. She's cute. Did she give them her
phone number?'

'I don't know. Do you want a swap? She
doesn't do nothing for me.'

Above the morgue door, the duct
gurgled. Thin yellow liquid sprayed from
join. The porters jumped back. The trolley
stayed where they were.

'Oh shit.'

'Or piss. Why don't they do a proper
mending job?'

'They'd have to replace the whole lot.
Cheaper to patch it up as they go.'

The porter with the armpits and his
replacement trolley went behind the
morgue door.

The next porter to roll Angela rolled her
very slowly.

want to have babies with you straight
ay,' he said.

he breathed his odour closing in. No
en hallucination. He was probing his
v inside her mouth but only as far as her
:rap teeth.

:ome on! Relax!'

You won't get any babies out of me,'
ught Angela, 'unless if you're lucky I
ght start hatching some of those ectopic
osaur eggs.'

hey were at the end of the tunnel and
other lift.

Jp

he doors opened into a vault without air.
Shall we do some sight seeing? I want
nake you happy so I'm going to give
 a Christmas present.'

ears pushed out from behind her eyes.
:'d never sobbed from behind closed teeth.
Oh God,' she thought, 'I'm losing it.'
he didn't push out hot melting
hions. She spurted. Her tears gobbed.
: turned her eyes towards him.

'I'm sorry, I'm going to have to save my
present until after you've seen the priest.'

In keeping with the true sense of occasion
the lift opened after moments of piety.

The lift opened next to the confessional.
This was what they'd call queue jumping.

The organist swayed in her blue floral
dress, a sleeveless 'Jesu Joy of Man's
Desiring'. A full congregation and they
were sweating. A sauna to begin the
process of toxic release. To each
confessant a nurse was assigned or was it
a porter?

Into the wine velvet folds of the
confession booth Angela's porter pushed
her trolley hard. Behind the weight of the
folds, his pitbull grill, his bullet proof glass
the priest glanced down onto what he was
dealing with. A glance not long enough to
include Angela. He profiled his head
towards his collar fan.

'Good evening Derek. How nice to see
you again. You're doing a good job. Pursue
the path of service and you'll find real inner
serenity. Would you like to say something
about your eating disorder Derek?'

to be continued

BY ROBYN CONWAY

SKY SO BRIGHT, think at first its a fly that won't g
away, but it's a floater. You know, like when you point a video at
the sun and the camera gets burnout. My one used to look like
bubble but it's gone black now. You're not meant to get them
this young – guess I spent too much time wearing crap
sunglasses 'cos they looked good.

Days like this remind me of greece. Whites whiter than, so
you squint against the sun, scuttle outside and lay there
feeling it warm your skin, so horny you could fuck the first
builder that walks by, the first rockabilly boy on the dole wit
a big shiny quiff and meaty muscles, the first one with all h
hair in the right places.

Isn't it funny Mark says, how women always go for fat o
bald guys with pots of money. Mark washes his
hair every day and plans to be poor when he's old. He to
me the theory one time, stimulating the follicles or
something, I can't remember, but so far it's working. H
twentyeight now, same age Panos was when I met him.
I'm twentyeight too, five years older, five years more
wasted, five years less to live.

At the beginning I knew Panos was something to
push away with a long stick, not get close to. But bac
then I thought no
one could get
within miles of
me. Even living
with the guy
didn't count.
What I liked
best was being
in his apartment while he was out at work, takin
showers or trying on clothes and make-up left
behind by old girlfriends. Or driving round soft
Athens sidestreets late at night in the open top
Plymouth. Scrape of metal as we turned a corr
into some little square bright with allnight caf
and openair cinema. Afternoons when the
melon truck came round, buying them by the

o off the back of the pickup, swinging them home in plastic bags. When you
acked open the green shell, shock of cool red juice running down your throat.
ever tasted this good in england.

Days like this I cycle to the greek shop on seven sisters, buy sweet peppers and
iny black aubergines, bunch of dill with no plastic round it, and cook meat fresh
om the butchers instead of some fake exotic dish from Waitrose.

The stuff that brings it back is always the good stuff, the weather, the sex, the
sconnected freefloating colours in that blinding light. Never the craziness that
nt me back here clutching at england's solid grey pavements and neonfronted
ops, hiding under a blanket of cloud in damp brick rooms.

That other stuff belongs the year I got burned. Twentyfive, the year I almost
ecked out, without even meaning to. Three years on, and I still can't tell about it.
Oh, I can tell you how I got thin and then thinner than thin, how the heat that
ar went on right through September and October, and people with bad hearts
ed from eating hot meals in the middle of the day. How the chemist looked
nny at me when I went to buy over-the-counter speed, but sold it me anyway,
en muttered something I didn't catch on my way out. How I ate nothing but
elon and yogurt, cherries and nectarines, and I can't remember sleeping all
mmer. Most nights we had the mattress on the balcony and we lay there nude
th just one sheet. We were on the top floor, and fucked loud with no one to hear.
I left when I could pick out the text on the billboards, when I began to know what
ople would say before they said it, when I understood the football on the radio

RNOUT

d the taxidrivers and the old lady in the bakers. And I understood that I was just
other woman who'd missed the plane home.

Days like this I look up at the clear sky with its two black dots, and I know my
dy wasn't built for that kind of heat.

Maybe one day I'll make up stories to tell Kiva, stories about the girl who flew
o close to the sun. Will they keep her safe and loved, or will she go out and get
rned anyway, just to see what it feels like?

by Pearl Delaney

THE HURT

Story: Ann Marie
Images: Oliver Manton

The day of the dinner was a disaster, she was late going home, the computer went down and she lost a week's work. The dinner was meant to be just the girls, dial out curries and chocolate, wine and cigarettes, giggling and whinging. But Jade made an excuse to stay home, said he was ill...

Shit! He's home, and I've forgotten the tinfoil.

Hold my head

We'll trampoline

Finally through the roof

Velouria!

The smell of her home, of concre and city dirt, of the post-war bui ing, greeted her like an old flame The apartment was full of smoke, like clouds out an airplane windo Many small balls of tinfoil – they' been at it all afternoon.

he wine was half gone and there was a pile of blood-sodden tissue. Jade had had other blood nose. The cat had eaten half the cheese and been sick on the vegetables.

eisa pulverised tiny white lumps with a phone-card. He piled a mound powder onto glass covered with tinfoil, jabbed holes in it.

She shook her head and glared at him.

He stayed and shared the curry with them. Her friends screwed up their faces as Jade got curry sauce around his mouth and in his hair. No-one relaxed, enjoyment was only for the sadistic.

hen they left, he hunched over the glass again, the lighter flame flickering, filling the om with white plastic smoke.

hen he offered the glass she took it.
r heart increased its output and her
lms sweated.

She wanted to be where he was, to find him again,

but he was too far gone.

rough the black lace
rtain it was possible to
unt the stars, and the
on dribbled down, she
ard the cat in the fridge.

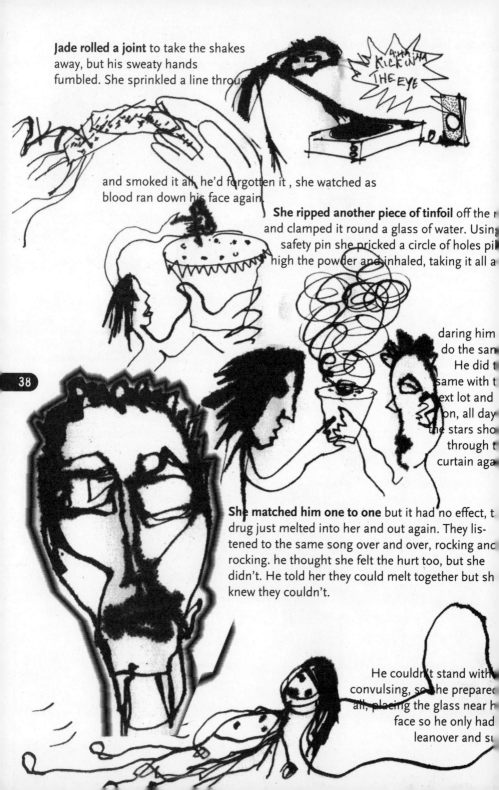

Jade rolled a joint to take the shakes away, but his sweaty hands fumbled. She sprinkled a line throu[gh]

KICK IN THE EYE

and smoked it all, he'd forgotten it , she watched as blood ran down his face again.

She ripped another piece of tinfoil off the r[oll] and clamped it round a glass of water. Usin[g a] safety pin she pricked a circle of holes pi[led] high the powder and inhaled, taking it all a[way]

daring him [to] do the sam[e.] He did t[he] same with t[he] [n]ext lot and [s]o[o]n, all day [as] the stars sho[ne] through t[he] curtain aga[in.]

She matched him one to one but it had no effect, t[he] drug just melted into her and out again. They listened to the same song over and over, rocking and rocking. he thought she felt the hurt too, but she didn't. He told her they could melt together but sh[e] knew they couldn't.

He couldn't stand with[out] convulsing, s[o s]he prepared [it] all, placing the glass near h[is] face so he only had [to] leanover and su[ck]

...he just piled up the drug and gave it to ...m, and **the cat pulled everything out of ...e fridge onto the floor**. The milk ...nelled bad and the telephone rang, ...de shat in his pants, no-one noticed.

He turned his dreadful blue eyes on her gratefuly, lovingly
then they rolled back in his head.

...e got up and surveyed the filth
...ound, smelling him, herself and the
...tpiss for the first time.

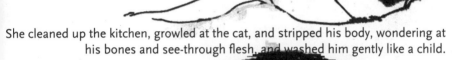

She cleaned up the kitchen, growled at the cat, and stripped his body, wondering at
his bones and see-through flesh, and washed him gently like a child.

...e wiped the floppy rubber lips, th...
...sed him, tasting him for the fina...
...ne. A long hard kiss, clash of teeth...
...arching for the tongue that was still
...t quite cold.

After this she didn't know what to do.
**She supposed she should call an ambu-
nce,** but first she rang Cheiko asking her
to dinner on Thursday.

The first time Mickey saw one of the creatures, he was waiting to change at Euston. The station tiles were yellowed as dentures.

He stood on the grimy white strip at the platform edge. From a low gap across the track, a stubby clawed hand poked a stick to fish through the litter scattered on the line.

Mickey glimpsed a small greenish face before a train hurtled across and screeched to a halt.

"Fuck, did you see that?" he said to the people by him. They mostly looked away but a schoolgirl in leather lowered her comic and said, "What?"

"There was a funny little face down by the line."

She sniffed. "Oh. Molemen; they're everywhere. Didn't you know?"

The tube doors took abreath and slammed open. People pushed impatiently past one another to get off or on. "But where do they come from?" wondered Mickey.

The girl said, "A friend of mine says the Underground use them to dig their really deep tunnels." She shrugged and got into the tube.

Mickey shook his head. "Weird."

He waited for the doors to close. The train moved off, fitfully at first and then more surely, finally rushing past and away down the tunnel, its wind sucking at his hair and flapping his clothes; and when it was gone he crouched to peer across the tracks; but there was nothing to see except a gap in the yellowed tiles.

LURID

by Michael River

Dogboy pressed his head against the locked door in darkness, straining to make sense of the muffled voices [out]side. "He's in here," said his father, [an]d a key clinked in the lock.

A bare bulb spasmed to life. The door [sw]ung open and they came in; his father [lar]ge and solid, the other man shorter but [jus]t as wide; ugly face, an overcoat. "[Je]sus, what a stink," said the stranger, [wri]nkling his nose. His father grunted. "[Th]ink the little bastard will wait to piss [wh]en he's told?"

[Th]e room was filthy. The blackened [wal]ls had survived small fires; scraps of [foo]d, rubbish and shit littered the floor. [Th]e stranger stepped carefully over the [deb]ris and crouched by Dogboy. Dogboy [squi]rmed into the corner, shying away [fro]m him.

His father clouted him, seized the [lea]ther strap of his muzzle and forced his [an]gry face upwards. "Be polite, you little [shi]t," he growled.

The short man gave a low whistle. "[W]here did he come from?"

"His mother." His father spat. "That [sl]ut. My guess is she got herself screwed [by] some dog. She always liked animals. [Or] more likely a rat; one of those giant

rats that live in the sewers. Like you see in the papers, even bigger than dogs, with fat greasy haunches and yellow teeth long as your finger." He paused, licked his lips. The thick tip of his tongue was grey.

Liar! It's not true, Dogboy wanted to shout, but all that came out was a kind of gnnyaaring noise, a wordless bleat. His father said, "See what he's like? I told you." He shook his head; his fat jowls wobbled.

"I need to see his teeth," said the other man.

"Okay." His father bent to undo the muzzle. "Not a sound," he warned Dogboy. "And you better fucking know I mean it." The muzzle flopped on the floor. Dogboy stretched his jaws and the short man grabbed them, holding his mouth wide open.

"I done what I could for him; fuck knows I tried. Not that the little shit has ever been grateful." He spat again, a thick gob that smacked wetly on the wall by Dogboy's head.

The stranger nodded and made understanding murmurs. He finished his inspection and stood. "Shall we call it eighty quid?"

41

Dogboy's father shook his head as he refitted the muzzle. "A hundred. It would have to be a square hundred."

"Okay." The man pulled folded notes from inside his coat, counted them out.

You bastard, thought Dogboy helplessly.

3

Mickey met Lisa at a party in a swampie squat off some road in Hackney. She wore rainbow striped jeans and an oversize fawn jacket with sheepskin lapels. They talked drunkenly, leaned close until their legs were touching and went home together.

While he was searching out clean glasses in the kitchen, she gave a yelp from another room.

"There was a big lizard in the wardrobe," she told him.

"His name is Darwin. Shit." The glass panel fronting the wardrobe was ajar; the ledge deserted.

They hunted about for quarter of an hour before finding him wedged in behind a radiator. Mickey tried to pry him out but he scrabbled back out of reach, toes clicking on the metal bars, and wouldn't budge.

"He goes for the warmth," said Mick "This country is too cold for him really."

"It's too cold for most of us," she sai

On the bed they took off each other's clothes. His prick rose to the touch of h hand; her fingers charmed it.

"Doesn't the noise of trains ke you awake?" she asked.

"You ge used to it There aren't that ma through the night."

In the morning they woke to find Darwin lying between them legs splayed stiffly out like he w a piece of badly stuffed furnitu eyes black glass marbles in his leather snout.

4

The car was massive; a subterranean rumble propelled it down the street. Dogboy sat in the back. Grills covered the windows. The wide leather seat was webbed with hair-fine crack stiff with age.

They crossed a bridge and drove alongside the riv for a while.

Dogboy pressed his face to the glass between the bars to see the rolling band brown water, the Thames conveying rubbish relentlessly down through the c Grey cloud hung still in the sky and the city lay submerged under an aquatic

oom. His
eath soon
gged up a
tch of glass.

The short man
anced back from the wheel, swore and
ffed his head. "Get down, you stupid
cker," he said.

Dogboy cowered back in the seat.
isten," the man said after a minute, in a
othing tone. "You know, you don't have
 worry about me; I'm not going to hurt
u. I'm here to help. Things have
anged for you; yeah, they've changed for
e better. Things are looking up."

He smiled widely. Dogboy could see his
ings glint in the rearview mirror. "The
me's Eddie," said the man, and stuck
s hand back over the seat. Dogboy
ared dumbly at it, hanging in the air with
gers half spread.

5

ickey liked to watch the cables on the
nnel wall as the train dived deep
tween stations.

He liked the way they wove serenely
ross one another and back, cables all
e different colours of the Underground
ap; Circle yellow, Metropolitan mauve,
cadilly indigo, District Green... And then
e sudden bright blur of a platform
ulling alongside, people stepping
rward, the doors drawing breath before
ey slammed open. Mickey loved the

tube, everything about it except grey snot.

Coming out at Tufnell Park, he noticed
a lurid kind of light from the sky. He saw
the notice among flyers papering over a
derelict shop. It was small and badly
photocopied:

TONIGHT

SEE MOLEMEN FIGHT!

ALL ACTION, ALL FUN!

BETS TAKEN

PHONE FOR LOCATION

and a phone
number. Mickey frowned, and carefully
peeled the flyer loose.

6

Eddie dumped Dogboy in a 40-gallon
drum. Dogboy yelped at the icy touch of
the water. Fine brown hair fanned out
from his torso. Grey grime sloughed off
under the scrubbing brush and floated
on the water, curds and whey, mouldy
peeled rinds.

"You've got to think of this as a career,"
said Eddie, scrubbing energetically.
"Think big! It's the only way to get
anywhere in life. Take advantage of what
makes you special."

I don't want to be special, thought
Dogboy. He sneezed and wiped his wet
snout. There was an old cracked mirror on
the wall by the drum. In its surface, his
face, brown velveteen, was cut into odd
fragments, jigsaw pieces. He tilted his

head, trying to fit the pieces into a face more like other people's.

"Wait, let me get you something," Eddie said. He hunted through a bin of odds and ends and came up with a spiked leather dogcollar. "Great for your image."

Well, thought Dogboy, giving up on the mirror, maybe at least the food will be better. He let Eddie fit the collar round his neck.

7

Mickey bought a paper from the stand outside the tube and hurried through belches of rain to the smudged window of the cafe. He ordered a coffee. While the woman used a hissing machine to lay a carpet of dirty flocked white fizz over it, he eyed rows of sagging yellow pastries under the glass counter, wrinkled donuts shedding sugar like dandruff.

He spread the paper out by the window. The table rattled when a train passed overhead, tinkling the ashtray, cup and saucer, setting the sugar bowl jiggling, jogging on the spot. He sipped his coffee, gagged and set the cup down, pushing it to the furthest corner of the table.

Bold headlines jammed the front page:

MP BUGGERS BABY
QUEEN'S SECRET LOVE DUNGEON – EXCLUSIVE

"Hi, I'm late," said Lisa.

"It's okay. I was reading the paper. Have that coffee if you want."

They sat watching traffic in the rain, Lisa flipping sugarcubes out the door with her teaspoon whenever the woman behind the counter looked away. An old dosser lurched past the window, his feet wrapped in plastic bags. "Look at that rain," said Lisa. "Why did you come here anyway, Mickey?"

He shrugged. "Sure don't know why I stayed. This isn't an easy place to get to know. It's like there's some kind of secret society you have to get initiated into."

"I'm not sure I get you. Like what?"

"Well, for instance; d'you know anything about the molemen?"

"Huh? Where's that?"

"It's not a place; they're little sort of creatures that live underground." His ear reddened. "Look, I know it sounds ridicu—"

"Molemen, oh sure. It's your accent. Sure I know about the mole-people." She shrugged and dropped the spoon. "So what's the big deal?"

"Do you know where they come from?"

"I heard it was something to do with the old plague pits. You know, during the Black Death they dug these giant pits and st dumped bodies in them and earthed em over. Maybe some of the bodies weren't dead yet, maybe they survived and even had babies and stuff. It's more than four hundred years ago now. Is it important?"

He dug through his various coat pockets, came up with a tattered flyer, unfolded it and spread it smooth on the yellow formica. "Look at this. What do you think?"

"Sounds disgusting. You want to go?"

Eddie and Dogboy were let in through an unmarked side door and left in a room stacked with chairs and desks, a bulb swaying ill-at-ease from the high ceiling.

A man came in to inspect Dogboy; his teeth leered huge and yellow through a magnifying glass. His eye swam across like a pallid fish going belly-up.

"Well?" said Eddie.

"Looks okay," the inspector admitted.

"Sure he's okay," said Eddie, and slipped him a fiver. "Hey, is this a beauty contest or what?" When the inspector had gone he paced the room. His shadow swung wildly around the walls, tethered loosely to the lightbulb.

"Wait here," he decided. "I'll go check

out the competition for you."

Under-lit orange clouds swarmed across the sky over Shadwell. Mickey and Lisa got lost for a while among marching council estates, grim redbrick regiments, as they tried to match the tangle of real streets to the neat lines of the A-to-Z. They followed alleys between enormous hangars housing fleets of stolen refrigerators and videos.

Finally they found it, down by the river; an iron staircase bolted to the side of a warehouse leaning over the mudflats. The water caught streetlight like tight-stretched clingfilm.

The bouncers eyed them over, let them through. Mickey bought tickets and they entered a narrow corridor, following it down to a large room, hot and noisy, filled with smoke-blue air, the smell of beer, sweat and cigarettes. By the ring a line of touts were taking bets.

Lisa looked across the crowd and saw a man leaning in a doorway, talking and waving his hands about. "Hey," she told

45

Mickey. "I got to go to the loo."

"Again? But you went just—"

"I think my period's starting. Get me a drink?" She pushed off through the crowd. Mickey made his way through to the thick of the bar and ordered a couple of beers.

10

Dogboy put on his collar and practiced fierce growls in the mirror. When the door swung open he looked up expecting Eddie, but a woman's head poked around its edge instead. Her dark hair was knit into ragged dreads.

"Hi," she said, looking around the room. "Sorry, I was looking for the toilets." She had a book in one hand. On the cover, yellowed palazzos rippling under water; Calvino's Invisible Cities.

Dogboy cleared his throat. "That'th one of my favourite bookth," he said gruffly. "'Thitieth, like dreamth, are made of dethireth and fearth, even if the thread of their dithcourthe ith thecret...' Uh, I don't remember the retht."

She looked at him more closely, dropped the book, stooped to pick it up. "Oh. Yeah, I just started it, don't know yet." She hesitated. "My name's Lisa."

"Hi."

She came right into the room. "They were talking about you outside, about the fight. You been doing this long?"

"Not tho long... Thith ith the firtht time acthually."

She shook her head. "If you don't mind me asking, why are you doing it?"

Dogboy scratched his muzzle. "I worked in a thircuth one time, and that wathn't tho good. The animal tamer wath a right bathtard. I ran away to home in the end. My father wathn't pleathed; they thent the thtrongman around to get thome money off him."

"Look, I got to go. If you want, look me up. I haven't got a phone but I'm squatting this lock-up near King's Cross, you could look for me there." She found a pen in one of her pockets but no paper.

"Write it on my hand," said Dogboy.

11

"You're not from round here, are you?" said the man next to him; skinny and shaven-headed, his inaccurately tattooed neck like a plant's blue-leafed stalk.

"Um, yeah, I am. I've just been overseas for a while."

"Don't matter to me. You like it here, then?"

12

Mickey gulped from his
~~gl~~ass and set it down.
~~L~~ondon? I don't know.
~~I~~ mean, what is there to
~~lik~~e?"

The other man
~~sh~~ook his head. "Ah, but
~~it'~~s always poisons that
~~ar~~e addictive isn't it?
~~Ev~~olution fucked up, you
~~kn~~ow what I mean? Now
~~pe~~ople like what hurts
~~th~~em. There might be no use
~~in~~ it, but that's the way
~~th~~ings are." He worked a
~~fa~~g out of his pocket and lit up.
~~W~~ho're you fancying for
~~to~~night then? I'll give you
~~a~~ tip; go for the new one,
~~th~~e 'dogboy'. These
~~m~~olemen aren't so
~~h~~ot."

"Where do you think they come from?
~~T~~he molemen."

"Eh? Oh, it's always been a good place
~~to~~ hide out, underground, hasn't it? I
~~sh~~ould think they're the offspring of
~~c~~riminals gone into hiding, ex-Nazis and
~~th~~e like. A few generations and they'd
~~c~~hange to suit the tunnels; that's
~~ev~~olution, know what I mean?"

Coming out the door into the
corridor Lisa bumped into Eddie.
"Who— Hey! Lisa!" His wide face
split in a surprised grin. "Where
have you been?
How did you
find me?"

She sighed. "I didn't
find you. I wasn't looking. What
are you doing here anyway?"

"Business. You know. Are
you here with anybody? Not
that Bhrama bloke, is it?" He
looked apprehensive.

"No, that's distant history."
Some people jostled past.
Eddie took her arm and she
shrugged him off.

"Baby, why didn't you
call me?" he asked.

"Look, Eddie. We tried; it
didn't work. These things happen."

"But I thought–" said Eddie.

"Unlikely." She kissed his cheek
quickly. "I really have to go. See you
round."

13

The tip-off had come anonymously, a
voice calling out of the muffled rumble of
a public phone booth. Inspector Patel
rubbed his hands together, trying to work

some warmth into them. His men shuffled around in the alley, anxious, bored.

"Can't we go in, Chief?" asked one of them. "It's fucking cold."

"Not yet. We wait for them to start." Patel paced across the mouth of the alley, peered around the corner to the closed door across the street.

"Okay if I play my gameboy?"

"If the volume's off. Now be quiet."

The ticking minutes were slow, sluggish in the cold. There was commotion from inside the building.

"That's it!" said Inspector Patel, jumping to. "In we go."

"Shit! And that was my highscore."

They ran across the street, under harsh halogenic clouds slowly breaking up.

"Go get 'em, champ," said Eddie, and pushed him through the door.

Dogboy stumbled into the ring. The crowd howled; bright lights glared down on him, singled him out. Sawdust scuffed over the ring floor. There was a weird reek from the large wire cage on the edge of the ring. Black shadows cross-hatched the stunted figures of two molemen crouched inside.

The trap door flipped up and the molemen burst out in a berserk panic, squealing in some secret tongue. Their soft wrinkled skin had a greenish tinge and was almost hairless; in the centre of

their foreheads grew a small lump, a sort of luminous bump, pulsing sickly light with each hoarse breath.

And I thought I was weird, said Dogbo to himself.

15

Mickey went pale. He sat back in his chai so he couldn't see; but the image floated lurid in his head, blinking like neon; the two molemen clamped by their teeth to the dog-boy, all tussling in the sawdust, scratched and bloody.

He forced his way through the crowd down to the ringside, where the touts wer still taking bets.

"I want my money back," he shouted through the uproar.

"Fack orff," snarled the tout and Micke hit him.

"Cops!" shouted somebody and the crowd moved as though a switch had bee flicked, sweeping him away. Lisa grabbed his elbow. "Come on, we're getting out of here."

Dogboy paused on the windowsill to take a breath and jumped. He somersaulted through cold night air. Patches of cloud and stars and their reflections in the river all whirled up together, a dim kaleid-

scope. He splashed and sank in a
stream of bubbles, felt rough mud
under his feet and kicked up. The water
was icy, cold to the bone. He broke the
surface shivering.

"Hey!"
shouted Eddie.
Help!" His
head and shoulders were stuck in the
window. He strained to pull himself through.
From behind hands seized him, and,
swearing, he disappeared from view.

Red and blue lights wheeled
across the side of the building.
Dogboy set off paddling for the
orange and silver glitter of the far
bank. Ink letters blurred on his hand as it swept through the water,
blurred and ran away.

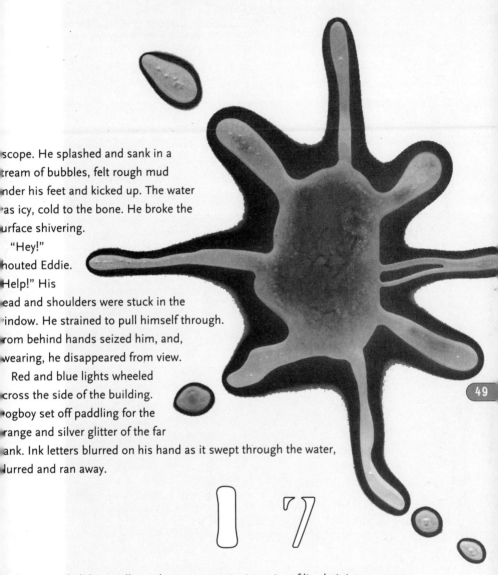

17

Mickey sprawled dejectedly on the mattress, tipping a jar of live bait into a saucer
on the floor. Darwin watched with one eye; swivelled the other to study Lisa sitting
on the window sill.

"What is the matter with you?" she said.

"They got away!" wailed Mickey.

"I should hope so, too!"

"Sure; I mean— I'm glad. But before I could get a really close look at them." He
shook his head. "And that dog-boy; I wonder where he came from?"

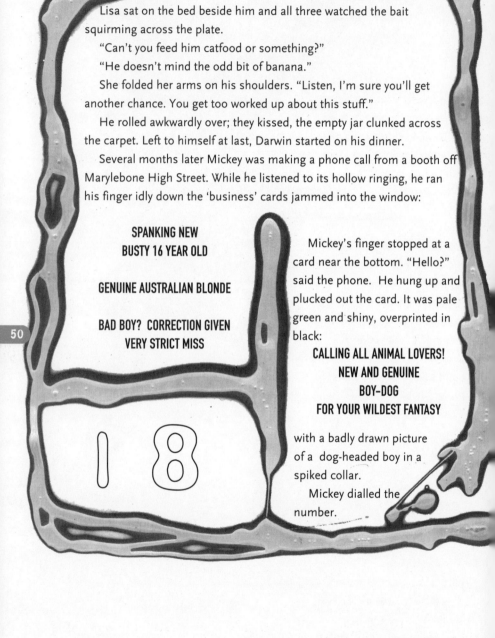

Lisa sat on the bed beside him and all three watched the bait squirming across the plate.

"Can't you feed him catfood or something?"

"He doesn't mind the odd bit of banana."

She folded her arms on his shoulders. "Listen, I'm sure you'll get another chance. You get too worked up about this stuff."

He rolled awkwardly over; they kissed, the empty jar clunked across the carpet. Left to himself at last, Darwin started on his dinner.

Several months later Mickey was making a phone call from a booth off Marylebone High Street. While he listened to its hollow ringing, he ran his finger idly down the 'business' cards jammed into the window:

SPANKING NEW
BUSTY 16 YEAR OLD

GENUINE AUSTRALIAN BLONDE

BAD BOY? CORRECTION GIVEN
VERY STRICT MISS

Mickey's finger stopped at a card near the bottom. "Hello?" said the phone. He hung up and plucked out the card. It was pale green and shiny, overprinted in black:

CALLING ALL ANIMAL LOVERS!
NEW AND GENUINE
BOY-DOG
FOR YOUR WILDEST FANTASY

with a badly drawn picture of a dog-headed boy in a spiked collar.

Mickey dialled the number.

CATATONIC

Caroline Pretty

Tom often wished that he was a goldfish. It was not so much the thought of
a secure environ-ment with regular feeding times that appealed, but more the
seven-second memory capacity.

'What are you thinking about?' his current partner demanded.

Tom screwed his serviette into a ball and placed it on top of the half-eaten pasta.
'Not much really,' he mumbled, and lit a cigarette. Other conversations intruded as
Tom watched the fine smoke lines separate and curl into the air around him. After
several minutes he looked up and spoke to her half-averted gaze.

'Do you think that life would be much easier if you were a candle?'

'What do you mean?' she ventured, flicking ash into the foil dish between them.

'Well, you would either be one... or
nothing,' he said slowly. 'There's no half-state, is there.'

She stubbed out her cigarette and sighed. 'Tom, you're geeking out again. You need
to sort yourself out.'

But Tom knew she was wrong. Yesterday he had caught himself living the sort of life
he had dreaded falling into, and now he couldn't bring himself to make the effort to
change it. After a couple of catatonic hours he had come to the conclusion that
reality was an out-dated concept and that it was to be bypassed at all costs.

'What do you think about general shrub-life?' he asked quietly, staring into her huge
concave eyes as he bobbed around in the weeds.

the Idler

THE ONLY MAGAZINE

DEDICATED TO LOAFERS,

LOUNGERS, LOLLYGAGS

AND EVERYONE WHO

LOVES TO *live life*

in the slow lane

ONLY £1.50 FROM SELECTED

NEWSAGENTS AND BOOKSHOPS.

OR CALL **0424 755 755** TO

TAKE OUT A SUBSCRIPTION.

Hot sex
Raw sex
Wrap it up and buy it
sex.
Dial now sex
Dirty sex
Cheap sex,
More sex

SAFER

THAN

safer than ever before
no fluids spilled,
no need to cum,
sex in a box, sex over
sex without moving,
sex without sweating
clean sex
sex over the phone.

raunchy
dirty
lusty.
sweat

through the receiver sex
over the phone,
I can feel your come in my throat,
down the phone sex,

ore than ever before
ex.
ım sex

safe sex

safer than ever before sex.
Put your condom on the handset,
place a dental dam on your face,
over the phone,
makes it safer than ever before
sex.

tit sex,
no kissing sex,
Dial now sex
No touching sex,
you can come sex,
own my throat,

I'll sit in your face sex,
you like my clit sex,

imaginative sex,

sex without lust
sex without visuals,
verbal diarrhoea sex,
sex costs you money sex,
sex over the phone
sex costs you money,
sex all alone.
sex in the street,
sex on the station,
sex with no-one knowing sex,
sex all alone,
over the phone,

53

EVER
by Michelle Baharier
BEFORE SEX

pussy
cock
dial now

sex, sex, sex, sex, sex, sex, sex, sex, sex, sex, sex.........................
keep calling.

Mrs Shuffleoff and the plank

Bertie Marshall

Brian O'Grady sits in the dim light of his Kings Cross bedsit, looking out of a greasy window onto the main road. Rothmans cig—red burn on index finger, a can of warm Tennents Super within grasp. He is only 3 hours away from his booking. 10.45pm at the InteStella Club.

At a snail's pace, Brian is becoming a cult figure on the London drag scene – not bad for an old dear pushing 60, in long exile from his native Belfast. Brian has created a persona, a drag turn called Mrs Shuffleoff, a drunken landlady based on his mother. Flower print polyester frock, slingback sandals and ash blond wig found in a builders skip, Brian has only one routine that he repeats twice a night: 60s pop star Susan Maugham's song **I wanna be Bobby's girl.**

Brian sits at the table by the window, waiting for the day to pass. Rothmans graveyards, empty beer cans pile up. He turns and catches himself in the mirror: ruddy face, balding, big bulbous eyes like a goldfish and as he gazes he hears a voice say 'is anyone there?' Pulling himse together he staggers over to the record player and puts on a record... **Ladies and Gentlemen, the London Palladium is proud to present, Miss Dorothy Squires.** The recorc is full of yells and the overture repeat over and over like a sustained soundtrack from a nightmare. No singing just applause, applause, applause. The needle stuc in the groove.

Brian takes several curtsies and a bow. Suddenly inspired, he rushes to a cupboard and pulls out a livid pink feathe boa, draping the flightless fowl around hi neck. Taking another bow, tripping the light fantastic, tumbles to the floor. Result. Sprained ankle. To mask the ache in his Achilles Brian cracks open a final Tennents Super.

The clock spits the hours away, until it's time to call a cab for his first booking. He scrambles together his drag paraphernali

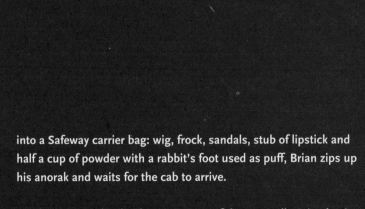

into a Safeway carrier bag: wig, frock, sandals, stub of lipstick and half a cup of powder with a rabbit's foot used as puff, Brian zips up his anorak and waits for the cab to arrive.

In the converted toilet dressing room of the InteStella Brian begins the ascent to Mrs Shuffleoff. Young queers and drag queens swirl past in a riot of colours, alcohol and sibilance. Brian/Mrs Shuffleoff is set apart from the throng like some precious old ornament that one cherishes but never touches.

Another Tennents Super goes down, it's very nearly show time. Off with the jeans and anorak, on with the contents of the Safeway bag. Brian squashes his pudgy feet into honey coloured tights and beige slingbacks. The crowning glory is the wig in place. As Brian checks the mirror, a couple of young queers sitting on empty beer barrels snigger hideously...

'Something is missing,' he thinks. 'Mrs Shuffleoff, ain't ya gonna put any slap on?' says one of the queens.

'Oh!' says Brian, 'I knew something was missing.' Embarrassed now, his hand shaking as he tries to apply the red stub of lipstick, he goes close up to the mirror. Some nightmare truth screams back at him; he misses most of his lips but manages to outline his mouth. The effect is sad clown.

'Never mind,' he thinks, rabbit foot beats powder across his cheeks.

The young queens screech in horror at Brian's red gash and rabbit foot, and depart swiftly.

Brian alone. 'Mrs Shuffleoff,' he hears. Brian is in a cocoon of numbness blown away by beer. 'Come on dear, Mrs Shuffleoff,' snaps the voice on stage. **I wanna be Bobby's girl** blasts out of the speakers. Brian races on stage, the glare of the spotlight, the hiss of the crowd.

Mrs Shuffleoff stands centre stage, then shuffles left a bit then right and on the boom-boom of the drum Brian punctuate the beat by bashing with his fists, sagging tits, not false ones but the real thing, geriatric mammaries, his body a slag heap of pink puffy flesh. Sweat trickles down his forehead, causing the mascara to run into his eyes, lashes batting, drooping.

I wanna be Bobby's girl,
I wanna be Bobby's girl,
that's the most important thing to me.

Mrs Shuffleoff is mid-song now, but his mouth doesn't fit the words, there's a natural delay. The audience are appalled i a camp way, screaming wildly hysterical. Mrs Shuffleoff smiles, shuffling left a bit,

ght a bit, firing, delivering the goods,
od Bless and cherish her twisted heart,
ostick smeared on chin, feet squelching
tight beige sling backs. **And if I was**
obby's girl...

rian looks like a demented granny on
ome sort of hallucinogenic drug, an
oscene cartoon between lives, melting.
rs Shuffleoff crawls offstage, laddering
er tights, wig sliding down the back of
er head. Disco music blares out; the
rong heave onto the dancefloor.

rian back in the dressing room picks up
stray beer, gulps it down, he's enjoyed
mself which is all that matters. The
owery frock falls like a synthetic bouquet
the floor, Brian standing in his
nderpants and those beige slingbacks.
d. sad. sad.

s he turns to go to the bar, allowing a
o-minute lapse before he makes his
ntrance, standing in the doorway is a
oung man, about 6 foot tall, shaved
ead, sharp features, beautiful green deep
et eyes, wearing white jeans and black
nd cheater jacket, unzipped revealing a
hite muscled torso and flat ironing
oard stomach, skinhead replica of the

stature of David. The two Gay clichés meet
– the old queen and rough trade.

'I liked your song,' says the young man.

Brian looks around, thinking the guy is
talking to someone else, even though the
dressing room is empty. 'Oh,' says Brian.

'Yeah, it was my mum's favourite,' says
the young man. 'Wanna drink?' he offers.

Brian stares in disbelief, can't stop his lips
from rubbing together in expectation.

'Come on mate, I'll buy you a drink,' says
the young man.

Brian is living a dream as the young man
walks behind him through the crowd to
the bar, his immaculate torso blazing in
the ultraviolet disco light. Brian feels like
Liz Taylor with her own personal minder.
They stand at the bar, the young guy
fixates on Brian; it's as though he's
weighing up something, some option.
Brian thinks he's sex on legs.

'Name's Colin,' says the young man.

'Brian' says Brian.

'What! Not Mrs Shuffleoff?' laughs Colin, the cruel bastard.

'No dear, now are you going to buy your grandmother a drink?' says Brian, holding his own.

'You're not my gran,' says Colin viciously.

Brian looks but doesn't know what to say, totally in awe of Colin's physical perfection. Nearby a gaggle of vicious queens nudge each other, nodding and sneering like fishwives at the pair. The bell for last orders rings.

Brian has been playing multiple fantasies over and over in his head ever since Colin bought the first bevvy. All scenarios lead to the same conclusion – Brian getting buggered.

'Drink up ladies please!' shouts the landlord.

Colin and Brian are nose to nose in a drunken stupor.

Ten green bottles standing one the wall and if one green bottle should accidental fall, there'd be nine green bottles standin on the wall, sings Brian hopelessly out o tune, fumbling for his front door key. An ambulance passes.

Colin's eyes bore a hole in the back of Brian's head, which he thinks looks like furry egg.

The pair clamber up the rickety stairs to the bedsit. Inside Brian turns on a bare light bulb, Colin trips over the feather bo and crashes into a plank of wood used a a shelf. Tatty paperbacks, bottle of cough mixture, tube of denture cream and a jewellery box smash to the floor, the lid flips open and Carousel Waltz plays.

Colin, unhurt but wound up, flops onto th bed. Brian looks at the mess on the floor, goes to the fridge and retrieves two beers.

The pair are slumped on a little single be A police siren screams. Brian's fingers metamorphose into a crab shape and crawl sideways across the bed to Colin's crotch. Orange street light flames on Colin's clenched jaw, eyes shut tight, Bria tugs at the zip. 'No, wait,' says Colin,

crambling to his feet. He stands in front
f Brian. Brian sits up, little beatific smile
ckers across his face as he
atches. Colin unzips,
mbling, and pulls
ut a huge flaccid cock.
rian gulps. Colin waves his
ck about in front of Brian's face. Brian
l a quiver leans forward ready to take the
oppy cock in his mouth, when
uddenly **a shower of gold!** Colin
isses in Brian's mouth. Brian
utters and coughs and runs for a cloth.

ith his jacket off now and red leather
races over nipples, green eyes pointing
ightly inwards, a crooked grin cuts
olin's thin lips.

rian shrouded in a tea towel wipes the
eluge off. Out of the corner of his eye
olin spies the plank of wood. His mind
oes blank. Carousel Waltz plays,
natches of Bobby's girl twirl in his
rain.

Oh, um, not really my sort of thing Colin,'
utters Brian. 'Maybe you should go now.'

Nope, can't do that,' grunts Colin. 'I've
ot a job to do, and I'm going to do it.'

Brian swallows deeply,
stoops to close the lid of the
jewellery box – **Carousel Waltz**
stops. Colin's temples throb, a
tremendous pressure fills his head.
Muscles tense, blood rush, like he's about
to come...

The plank of wood crashes down on Brian's
crown, legs buckle, falls to his knees.

'Oh no,' he whimpers, blood oozing out of
the top of his head.

'Sing I wanna be Bobby's girl!' commands
Colin, bringing the plank down a second
time, knocking Brian's false teeth out in a
puddle of blood. Colin thinks they look like
seaside candy, pink and sugary.

'**I wanna be**... please...' Brian's mouth full
of blood. The plank comes down again
and again and again, spilling Brian's
addled brain about the room.

'I AM TEZCATLIPOCA Aztec god of
sacrifice,' screams Colin. Raving red, his
face now an ancient Aztec mask
grimacing, ballooning out of shape, eyes
sinking deep into the head. The room
hums with slaughter.

Brian's crumpled body lies twisted on the
floor, eyes frozen in bovine terror,
eyelashes clotted with droplets of blood.

'Let it all come down through time,' Colin
says very quietly. A fire engine
roars past, screaming an epitaph to one
of cabaret's little legends.

DREAMING

I invited 20 people to dinner,
I moved to suburbia,
I had my own green field,
I had to hide from the locals because they didn't like townies,
I dreamt that my Dad gave me a lift to Exeter,
and that I flew and landed an aeroplane that I flew around New York.
I dreamt,
because I enjoy dreaming
It is cheaper than the cinema.

I dreamt I was swimming in the sea,
and you were sitting in an arm chair above the water,
and sharks were swimming above me,
dreamt I grew a black tulip,
and that there were cauliflowers and broccoli all over my kitchen floor.
I grew brussel sprouts as big as breasts,

I dreamt of being a mermaid
I dreamt of swimming in a swimming pool in Bethnal Green,
I dreamt of being a mermaid swimming in a swimming pool,
I was with lots of children we were having lots of fun,
We were walking across green fields,
before that we were all in Bethnal Green,
I lived in a circular room,
I could see all the bridges from my windows
as my windows faced the river,

Michelle Baharier

My First Porn

I saw my first porno film at the age of 12 the same way I saw Charles and Di's marriage in the middle of the night and **The Monster from the Black Lagoon** in 3-D.

I went over to my best friend's condo. Anna had a color tv, a satellite channel and a divorced mother who didn't care how late she stayed up.

Dirty movies were a little riskier so she whispered down the phone lines, 'You wouldn't believe what they show after midnight! **Porno!**' and waited for her mother to go out of town for a weekend. Diana's white gown trailed behind her like every girl's dream in a live 3am broadcast, and we fumed over 3-D glasses that didn't really work.

We snuggled for warmth on the rough industrial grey carpeting on sleep-over nights in front of the blue tv glow while the Chicago lights tried to sneak in through the mini-blinds, and, finally, Anna's mother went out of town without sending her to her father's house in the suburbs.

We ordered Chinese from the **5-Star Chop Suey**, although it was really three lit stars and two burned out neon ones.

We hauled our binge in leaky brown paper bags down the dark street lined with two flat buildings that used to have basement windows before they were bricked. Like a lurking monster, Anna's courtyard building hung at the end of the street. We struggled through the entranceway that smelled of mothballs and marched through the hall with brown gravy dripping on our fingers and Chinese smell in our noses.

Anna threw the newspapers off the kitchen table onto the floor and arranged the white cartons as if she was figuring out an eating strategy in her head. Anna was round and short like a ball with greasy black hair that went curly when it got a parentally enforced perm and a thick thumb that had really been two thumbs when she was born. Doctors sewed it together. I was not svelte, but I was taller. Thick thighs expanded from my denim skirt, and my stringy dark blond hair was growing out of a feathered haircut.

Thumbs popped the white boxes open creating a cloud of warm steam above the table. A twist of a cap, and the Coke was fizzing and bubbling into

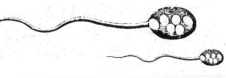

Donalds glasses. The egg foo yung went
forming pools of dark brown gravy on
plates and puddles on the table. Water
stnuts danced in the
p suey as the white-yellow sauce
ved into the brown gravy and the
nsprouts topped of the egg foo yung
ies. Our teeth crunched into wonton
through eggrolls that smelled of
hburger.
you think high school will be better
n seventh grade?' I said, mouth water-
as I dripped salty black soy on my
ssy plateful.
len,' Anna said, pushing a
rful into her mouth, 'it
to be.' Hanging
r the kitchen
ch, a dog clock
ed loudly and
ged its tail.
satellite chan-
wouldn't start
ming those
vies until mid-
nt. We stuffed our-
ves until we were
dy to burst, and then we
cked the fortune cookies let-
their hard sweetness try to clean our
ettes.
ant to show you something,' she said
her eyes lit up. She ducked into her
m as her paper fortune dissolved into
Chinese gravies on her plate. She came
with lace fabric draped down from the
of her head to the floor. 'Mom bought
r me. Now, I can really be Princess Di.'

She swirled like a top. 'Dress-up is for
kids,' I said. Her face fell but I didn't say I
was sorry.
I still want to be a princess.' The lace started to slide slowly down.
'You can't be a princess. You're Jewish.'
'I can be a Jewish American
Princess.' The lace kept
sliding down, and she
stood with her arms
crossed over her
chest that had
just needed a
training bra last
week.
'Dress-up is for
kids.' The lace
looked rough and
strong. It was
more like her moth-
er's than any princess's
lace. Her mother strutted
about in jeans and sneakers. Her hair
was always slicked back, and her shoulders were big. I turned to Anna: 'What do
you want to be when you grow up?
'A cook.' Anna's fingers ran through
her hair.
'I want to be a doctor.' I stuck my nose in
the air and Anna let go of the lace. It fell to
the floor, and Anna scooped it up into a

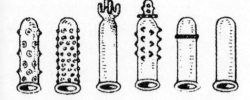

bundle and threw it into her room. 'Anna,' I said quietly as if afraid that someone in the next apartment would hear me. 'Have you seen these films before?' She shook her head. We settled on the couch sipping Cokes and tried to look like adults sipping sherry. Anna whispered in the blue tv light of the last 'real' movie of the night, 'I have heard about them.' With the fingers of one hand she formed a circle. With the index finger of the other she pointed and thrust into the circle. 'I heard they do that. Some of the films even have gays in them.'

Our lips were almost close enough to touch. 'I heard that gay men do it in the ass,' I said and looked around as if someone might be scribbling down my every word.

She shrugged her shoulders and explained knowingly: 'That's the only part that fits.' The credits rolled and a warning was sternly aired advising that the following programme was not suitable for minors and easily offended viewers. My scalp started to tingle.

This was more illegal than smoking.

A sandy beach filled the 19 inch screen with the title **Paradise Island**.

I giggled too and pulled the blanket tigh round me. Women paraded around in grass skirts and bikinis or even less befo my wide eyes. I felt a bit mushy betwee legs, and my hair started to stand on en bit my thumbnail and leaned forward un slid down to the floor. I burped before I could cover my mouth, 'Ooh, that was some Chinese food!'

'Oh Bob, I would never do something lik that,' said a blond to some guys shadow crotch. She was all lips, no teeth. She ha hips. Her breasts moved almost indepe dently of her.

'There's more,' Anna said as a bubbly blond from the tv said, 'I don't know wh you're talking about, Bob.'

Bob assured her that she did. Night fell the movie, and thin moonlight outlined curves of tanned female hips pressing against the naked whatever of some guy My nightshirt came down to my knees, a involved more fabric than was used for c tuming the entire female cast. Anna turr out the last of the lights, and the blue tv light was broken only by the occasional c headlight sliding past the window. We inched a little closer to each other.

'Bob, come on, we should talk.' Her brea were awfully round, and she stayed on h knees as she talked. Bob stood shirtless

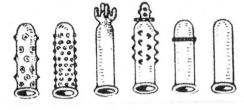

sun except for a light coating of oil.

s kind of stupid,' Anna said. 'It all

ms so fake.'

ghed. 'Yeah, I know.'

:an't do that, Bob,' the blond said in a

athy voice as she bent over.

e acting really sucks,' Anna said lean-

deeper into the couch.

ah. But it's kind of cool in a weird sort

way.'

ey never show the men's thing,' she

d. 'It's always in shadows.'

h yes, Bob,' the television said, 'more.

make it go in deeper.'

ou're right,' I said. 'It's not fair that they

n't show the men's stuff.' A guy named

ke walked across the screen wearing a

rfboard.

e stared into the blue light. The wind

nged against the windows. Water ran

isily through the pipes, but we kept

tching. Darkness closed in and opened

like legs and mouths with ruby red lips.

hy are so many of the women blond?'

na said, 'this is all so fake.'

ey, I'm blond,' I said and she gave me a

ok. 'Okay, so I'm not that blond.'

ob, Sandy and I are leaving.'

et out.' said Bob.

ndy and her friend, who was also skinny

d blond, sailed off into the sunset, sit-

g on the bow of a boat with their

easts dancing on their chests. they

ipped off their shirts making their

easts dance more. After some spy stuff,

or was it politics, they'd been kicked out of Paradise Island. Also, one of them wouldn't sleep with Bob. While one was very upset, the other said, 'Don't worry. We're young. We're in love. We have each other.

And then they did the unbelievable. They kissed **on the lips**. Their tongues even touched.

'Ewwww,' we said together turning to each other. We both feigned gagging, but neither of us wanted to lose our Chinese food.

'Ewwww! Yuck!'

We only watched one more film before drifting off to sleep. 'Anna,' I said as she clicked off the tv bringing quiet to the living room. 'Why are all the pictures hanging on your walls chalk drawings of nude women?'

We wrapped ourselves up in blankets next to each other, and Anna said, 'My mother bought them.'

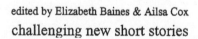

Submissions

are invited from *writers, graphic artists and comic artists*
of work suitable for inclusion in Pulp Faction's
compilations. What we are after is an exploration of the
title themes through fiction that is *original in form and
content*. Lengths from 500 words to 3000 words.

Future titles from the Pulp FACTION:

Technopagan   July 1995 (Deadline 21.April 1995)

Homeland   Nov 1995   (Deadline 1.July 1995)

Pulp FACTION is also interested any ground breaking writing
being hacked out there, including novels, which need not be
related to the themes listed.

Submissions (with sae)
to:
the Editor
Pulp FACTION
60 Alexander Road
London N19 3PQ

WHO WROTE THIS STUFF?

Ann Marie	traveller	destination unknown		London New Zealand
Barry Adamson	solo musician (Mute Records)	ex-bassist, the Bad Seeds		London/Australia
Joe Ambrose	edits Radio Alamut	Burroughs devotee		Dublin /London
Michelle Baharier	mixed media artist	play group worker		London
Darren Bennett	plays live keyboards in Cubanate		'61	South London
Robyn Conway	kinematomaniac, bibliobibendum		'69	NZ London
Pearl Delaney	late 20th C Luddite	astrologomancer	'62	London/Dublin
Victoria Stagg Elliott	writing serial killer book	collects tack	'69	Eng/Jewish/US
Kiran Grewal	reality escapologist	journalist	'59	all over the place
Paul Hamlyn	ex-accountant	travel crazy		North London
Richard Hayden	would-be aesthetician	in mid-life crisis		London
Sarah Jane	wants to live in NYC		71	London
Simon Lewis	life model with purple hair	lit crit student	73	Nottingham/Liverpool
Bertie Marshall	original punk, original drag	studies Chinese	71	English with Welsh bits
Paul Montigue	complacent attitude to cockroaches	fag	60	Brighton
Jacqueline Lucas Palmer	poet	loves Transglobal Underground	62	South London
Mathew Pitt	sells books in Camden	studies Film Theory		North London
Caroline Pretty	would rather remain an enigma		72	London
Michael River	survived plane crash in Madagascar	farms tropical fish	63	London
Lorna G Ruskin	studies arts	ex-nomad	63	Stoke on Trent
Helen Tookey	edits academic books	won't say who for	69	Sheffield

by Darren Bennett

Skin
of my Dead Mother

I wake from dreams that
my mother is dead. Lie
on my back in the cold
bed. The dream edges
tears from my eyes
though I know her death
is a fiction

I saw her four days ago, put the phone down to her mere hours before sleep. But I still cry.

I stand, look down at the bed. Only one body's indentation looks back at me. Lucy won't return for hours. I pick up her hairbrush from the bedside cabinet. It is knotted with her long blonde hairs. I untangle them one by one, remember the dream and the trail of childhood the dream tugged in its wake.

A mother astride a half-intered coffin. One foot on each side, toes amongst wet soil. Twist of mauve painted ingrowing nail. Smell of turned earth, worms, copulation, blood. A mother held frozen on a hospital bed. Forcing me outward, pushing me forward. A baby squirms, leaves the womb, and out into cold. The doctor cuts the umbilical cord, child wrapped and cast away.

In the bathroom, waiting for Lucy. Windows, half-open, catch the light.

My youngest memory is white walls and bare stone floor. Kitchen; my mother stooped, concertinaed. Sepia memory, mother in pony-tails and floral prints.

To be carried.

To be born.

From a mother who walked for nine months, me curled up inside her. I was born Caesarean, three weeks overdue. Mother did not want to shed me.

Curled up with Lucy in my head. Pressed to the floor gazing out of

s body. Standing by the pale wall. In the bathroom, stomach pressed
ainst the sink. Sink half-filled with stale water. Tiny hairs hung on the
-face. Spread across the bathroom floor. Plucking hairs from legs
h fingers. Four walls around me floor pressed below me ceiling
ove me unscathed.

By day Lucy works for her money. Home by night she gives it to me.
ait for her to feed me with coins. Can hear next door's television.
ughter. A priest asks for love and money. When he finishes a voice
els off murder statistics. I imagine Lucy placing her hands on the
evision screen. She has my mother's hands.

My mother's hands holding the child; she kisses its shallow pink
ad. The child is me, is of her body, the sum of one body slipping
wn on another, like my body slipping down on Lucy's. Mother's
nds are long and slender, like mannequin hands. Under the tap,
ter running over their backs. I am on the floor, and father standing
er me seems so big.

A click of the door and Lucy enters the room. Heels on the formica
or. Takes off her raincoat. Her face and clothes are frecked with rain.
'I'm wounded' she says.
'Where?'
She holds up her hand; the swollen thumb throbs the red of an
gorged penis.
'Caught it in the door at work' she says.

I take her hands in
mine, gaze at the thumb
then the rest of her
fingers. Split nail.
Graze on left index.

I kiss the swollen thumb. Want to suck it until the swelling subsides,
suck all the pain out.

'Come with me' Lucy says, and I follow her into the bedroom. Sit on
the bed and she stands there looking at me. She has slim hips and a

tongue too big for her mouth. She stoops, pushes her mouth against mine. Her skin is soft and warm. My hands find Lucy's spine, and she giggles.

'That's my weakness' she says.

And the last time I saw my mother I was on my way to meet Lucy. Lucy and me went to a restaurant in Leicester Square. The couple on the opposite table were arguing and he hit her and split her eye open and she bled all over the table cloth and the Chicken Kiev; I remember thinking, does Lucy know what it means to hurt, or does she only know the pain she can give?

On the bed Lucy shows me her other weaknesses; like the soft skin on the insides of her thighs, and how she cries at old photographs.

'I was married by sixteen' she says, and shows me the photographs. Sombre faces in dark suits and dresses. How many of them knew her stomach was filled with child?

'What happened to your husband? You've never told me.'

'You've never asked.'

'Yes I have.'

'Haven't.'

'Well I'm asking now.'

'Car crash, two weeks after the wedding. I hated him anyway.'

'So why did you marry him?'

'It seemed like the right thing to do at the time.'

'What about the baby?'

'I aborted it.'

She walks over to the window. Stares out, as if her dead husband stalks the streets below, hand in hand with the child that never was. Turns from the window, looks at me with eyes the colour of dead tongues. Shakes her lemon-coloured hair, removes her 'I Love New York' tee-shirt. Her body silhouetted against the sunlight reminds me of a shadow cast at mid-day by a sun so hot your skin is sore and you scratch it until it reddens and blisters. I hate the way she can undress when sunlight fills the room.

My face pressed to the floor. That is how Lucy wants me. Bare floorboards rough against cheeks. Splinters bleed me. Dust gathers in the corners of my eyes. I push myself around by raw knees. Two smeared red trails mark the places I have been.

She puts her hand under my chin, lifts my face up. Kisses the top of my head. Anoints me with her saliva. I peer up at her.

She opens my mouth,
examines me as if I were
a horse; turns over the
tongue, pulls back lips
and prods gums. Takes a
coin from her pocket. I
extend my tongue. She
places the coin on it. I
take the coin into my
mouth. 'This is the gift
of love,' she says

I feel the coin with my tongue, don't recognise it. Foreign, wafer-thin. Loose fluff.

Lucy sits on an old wooden chair; like the chair, she is spindly and sometimes seems to lack a spine. She covers my thin body with her hands. Touches my face while I look at her. Kisses me, her tongue lapping like a fishtail. I stare at her hands as she closes them around me. With every touch my nerve-ends shrivel and die like roses. She stands behind me so I can't see her, must trust her. I like the way that feels; power coupled with shame. Smell of rusty nails. My arms around her waist; appendix scar, line of tiny faint hairs running down her stomach. Her skin tastes coppery. When she touches me I forget who I am. She folds her body around me, takes me under her skin. The malaise of flesh, the curve of her contorted body on me; we are bonded together. I don't know where her skin ends and mine begins. I am buried under her skin, coursing her veins, breathing her blood. Choking.

When I am inside her she is so changed. I no longer know who she is, why I wanted her in the first place. Want to nullify us both, stare at her unfamiliar skin and no longer care about my own.

When we are finished we lay together in silence, a sweat-soaked heap. There is nowhere else to go. We need never move again. The first night I spent with Lucy we didn't make love. We just lay half-clothed in the darkness, kissing and touching. When day's logical light filled the room, I was almost embarrassed at how close we'd been. Perhaps if we'd had sex I wouldn't have felt that way.

I no longer own this body, am no longer inside it. I leave what is left under Lucy's skin. Oil and factory smells. Perhaps tomorrow we can go out together, and she can buy clothes and food and jewellry. All the things she can use with her money.

'This is the gift of love' she whispers, and laughs. 'When you were inside me I realised what makes you tick. You're obsessed with the worthlessness of your body.'

'Worthlessness?'

'Yeah. You despise everything physical, especially yourself.'

'I don't agree with you...'

'I'm not surprised. You don't even know who you are. If you did then you'd know you despise it. Why else do you refuse to undress unless the lights have been switched off first?'

'When are you going away?'

'Don't you want to talk about your problem?'

'When are you going away?'

'Sounds like I've struck deep...'

'When are you—'

'Stop changing the subject!'

Lucy stands, pulls stockings up her legs, her back to me now. I touch her spine, her weakness, but now she is not so weak. Finally she remits.

'In four days.'

'You still haven't told me where you're going.'

'What difference does it make?'

'I'd like to know. Are you seeing one of your other lovers?'

My hands shake. Hair falls into my eyes, repeatedly. 'Tell me about them. What are their names? Which one do you like best? How do they touch you? How do they fuck you? Do you prefer them to me?'

'Why should I tell you any of that?'

'Because I need to know.'

'Is that your way of ending them? By taking them away from me piece by piece?'

'No.' Nails bitten to nothing. 'It's just my way of measuring damage.'

'If you must know, it's... my father. He's ill. Yeah, very ill. He wants the whole family to be there. I don't know how long I'll be gone for.'

'So it could be weeks?'

'Yeah, I guess. I'm going out. Going for a walk, need some air, need to get out of this room. I'll be back soon.'

She stands in the doorway and we kiss. Her lips are sour. Next door's dog is barking.

'We all have our weaknesses' she says.

'Yeah. You cry at old photos, and I hate my skin.'

'One of these days I'm going to surprise you. You'll be naked in the middle of the room, and I'll throw on the lights. Then you'll have to look at yourself.'

Clean white grass. Born by the side of the road, or on the bank of the river. Lying in bed waiting for the sun to go down.

When Lucy returns we share laughter. The green and red bird tattooed on her shoulder where she likes to be bitten; with my penis inside her she runs her tears and snarls 'it's like slicing.' She splinters beneath my lips like glass and fragile bones and slithers of her pierce my skin and she says 'I can feel you.' She severs my veins and I am buried in her and I hate myself for depending on her and she does not care and my semen trickles inside her; she could hold a life inside her body, and I could do nothing.

In the room of our world I sit in silence as Lucy dresses. With each garment pulled on, each button fastened, the walls move in tighter. A storm hangs in the air, sour on the tongue, refuses to break. Lucy has a new eye-shadow, peach-pink. Her earrings a train of spirals, her shirt a forest of flowers; red, brown, blue. I like her best when she wears blue. She doesn't wear blue that much. If we both stayed here today we could choke on the dead air, die together on the bedroom floor, surrounded by clothes and bangles, that red-streaked pot plant, Dali prints and mother photographs. We need never leave again.

Lucy kisses me and leaves in the early evening.

'Just a few weeks' she says.

'Remember when you showed me that story?' I ask her.

This was a few days ago, one of Lucy's attempts at proving I didn'
love her; the story featured a couple heavy with the miracle of love. T
man wanted his lover so much he couldn't look at another woman ar
more than he could fly.

'Yeah, I remember' Lucy says. 'What about it?'

'It was so hard to tell you I felt that way about you.'

She shrugs. 'I'll call you soon.'

I stand by the window and watch her fade down the street. Giant
black sheets of rain hung from one horizon to the next like oceans of
blood. One of Lucy's leather belts draped over the back of a chair. I
pick it up. On the floor beside me a pair of her boots. I can't believe
these hands have ever held her. That I've lain beside her watching wh
she sleeps, her tiny eye-lashes, followed her around the bedroom and
picked up her clothes. I'd kiss the ground where she has walked, whe
she has left a taste of all she is; just to prove that I've loved her, that
she has breathed within my life. The telephone sits silent and gloats.
sloven orange nausea swells in me like a bee sting.

I sleep alone on the hard bed.

I lie awake.

I cover myself with my arms.

I am afraid.

In the kitchen. Know I
should eat. Haven't
eaten for days. Just
pour liquid into
myself and think
Lucy. I take a potato.
Cut it, put it in the
oven. Leave it there.

ake It out when the
utside Is hard and
he Inside Is soft.
tare at It. Poke It
Ith a fork.

Four little holes seeping steam. Before I met Lucy I'd ignore my stomach for days on end, ignore the empty gurgles that spurted in me until I could ignore them no more, until the hunger opened me with the precision of a surgeon. Visit the 7-11, buy crisps, chocolate, biscuits. Gorge until I become a corpulent mass of flesh and fat. Want to become the food, so others consume me and I can become nothing. I imagine my chewed body slipping through the intestines of friends and lovers; they draw from me what nutrition they can and the remains are shitted out.

I gaze out of the window. Cars glide by, rain on windscreens. A row of houses, met on one side by a stinking factory and on the other by wasteland. Windows, some boarded up, some dark, some lit yet their contents concealed by curtains. One window more or less opposite mine; I see a woman there. She stands by the window, hair black and very short like my mother made me have mine when I was eleven. Skin as pale as the walls around her. Covers herself with her hands. Hands first on her face, then her neck, shoulders next, breasts, down, over her stomach and out of my sight. The sequence replays like an immaculate ritual. Vase of yellow flowers on the window ledge.

I first met Lucy at a car crash. Last August. A Metro caught in the process of becoming a Cortina; polished chromium converges into one seamless skin. Bent lamp post. Screaming. Fat blonde mother; a bundle of cloth and skin held tight and bleeding in her arms. Crunching glass beneath stilettoed feet. Steam. Ambulances, white and red, and Lucy watching me watching the wounded. She sits on the kerb, sun on her face. Gazing into the gutter, the only person not watching two men carrying a stretcher to the awaiting ambulance.

As I proceed down the street Lucy follows me.

I go into MacDonald's for coffee and Lucy invites herself into my company. Blonde hair like ribs of corn.

'Nasty accident' she says. 'Crash.'

She runs a tea-stirrer across the soft back of her hand. I look from her hands to her face; a smile is hidden there.

'We're going to be lovers' she says. 'You have no choice, of course.'

Days pass by and on dark wet streets I am alone. Lines of black taxis like hideous beetles, and sometimes great raging torrents of rain; oceans, a deluge pounding the streets, followed minutes later by sunlight breaking out from clouds. Rain and sun alternate. Some days I follow people and imagine what their lives are like, or ride the underground and watch couples kissing. Lucy would never kiss me in public. Return home, sucked into aloneness. Must have left the television on; it now belches views to an empty room. Doesn't need an audience. The stillness in this room is like the months before I met Lucy. Every day return home from work, sit with records and words and watch the slow falling night, wait for it to pass so I can go to work again; my life outside work is a hollow where nothing happens. Sometimes after finishing work I delay going home, walk the streets, follow the stink of Fillet-O-Fish and newsprint, watch people and imagine being part of their lives. When I eventually do go home I swing open the door and my room is like a walk-in freezer where the ghosts of all those I have wanted and lost are lined up on meat-hooks along the walls. I walk through them, break off frozen limbs and hold them in my hands. But they no longer seem to matter, like browsing through the icons of somebody else's religion.

I am lying on Lucy's bed. Lucy poised over me. The only light is dust-perforated shards of sun that penetrate from between the curtains. She uncrosses her legs. Black stocking-tops and white thighs. Presses her tongue against mine. Her too-big tongue is thick inside. Raises her face, her fingers on my eyelids, closing them as if I were a corpse. Grips my arm, squeezes tight. When she releases it I see little red indentations where her fingertips were.

'This is the gift of love,' she whispers, briefly pushing her fingers into my mouth before retracting them.

As I slip off my clothes and lift the bed covers, Lucy puts out her hand and stops me.

'Wait' she says. 'I want to look at you.'

I stand naked before her, shivering like Christ recrucified.

'You like darkness, don't you?' she says, smiles and turns a ten pence piece between her fingers. 'Like hiding in it. Now this is to say that I love you...'

And her hand to my lips, opening my mouth, tucking the coin inside.

She smiles. 'Don't be afraid of power. What is wrong with self-hatred? You're beautiful. Now, into bed...' and she holds up the bed covers, open for me to slip between them.

One morning I am walking and listening to shouting children. In the distance behind rooftops a pillar of smoke aspires to the heavens, thickens and touches the sun. I follow the smoke, watch where it begins its course, am soon in a wide back street and there is the woman from the opposite flat.

Her back to me, black bag slouched across her shoulder as she leans against a garage door with NO LOITERING daubed on it in red paint.

Leggings clenched tight, left arm at right angle folded across her bag. Black rubbish bags. Beyond her flames escape through the roof of a house and climb skyward. Firemen with snakes for hoses battle with jets of water; blue jackets brilliant through smoke. I watch the woman as she watches the flames. Eventually she turns from the now dying fire, walks towards me. Stops, takes out a cigarette. A tiny purple scar dissects her right elbow.

'Do you have a light?' she asks. Her voice is like October.

I tremble as I take out a match, strike it, hold it to her; the wind blows it out and I strike another. She breathes on the cigarette, thanks me and walks out into the open street. I drop the match, watch her walk away. When I turn again the fire is extinguished; perhaps it only burne to lead me here.

All day I follow her through thoroughfares thick with people. As she walks she sways to a fictitious rhythm. I plot every move she makes.

She descends steps to the underground, evening light amongst rooftops, and shadow-like I hang to her.

On the crowded train I'm pressed as close to her as my fear allows. I could happily asphyxiate on her scent; honeydew and nicotine. I wish I could pull her close to me. Wish I knew how to use her. She is a surrogate Lucy. Black hair and her sleep-set eyes hidden behind wide tortoise-shell glasses, her physique like mine yet smaller; me in miniature. Her lips twitch. Black leggings and DMs. Her eyes are closed. I like this power, like the way it numbs me.

I follow her home and out again, and she walks through dark Soho streets. Turns towards the road, striking a match, lighting a cigarette, goes into a club and I go in there as well. Tightly packed bustle of chattering drinking bodies, smoke and a pulsating rhythm, a rainbow hair colours and I glimpse one or two faces from television. I order whisky and crouch by the edge of the dance floor, watch her as she dances.

Flower scrawled on her jeans. Her shoes are the same as mine. Floor scattered with fag-ends, ash and match sticks. Crushed pint glass.

Her hair shimmers as she moves. Her shirt is an ocean. Her feet move too fast for me. I wish I could slow them down. Want to worm into her, undo her buttons, snip a hole and climb behind her skin, lodge myself there; somewhere behind her breasts, somewhere near her centre. A man is spread out on the floor beside me, cartwheels of coloured light turning on is body. Wears a leather waistcoat that displays hairless chest and pierced nipples. Doesn't move. People step over him to get to the toilet. The woman dances against a wall, looks down at him. Every word I've heard surges inside me, forces my intestines aside and craves the air that lives dry in my mouth.

'D-do you know him?' I stutter.

She laughs, shrugs, nods, shakes her head, make-up thick like bruises around her eyes.

'Yeah. He's my... boyfriend.' She laughs again, stops dancing, puts her arms around me.

'I'm really stoned...' she breathes, pins me against the wall. Her mouth on my neck, her lips moist. Rush of hair. She looks into my eyes, touches my cheek. 'You look so innocent...' she whispers. Turns away, rasps wistfully 'That's a nice jumper. Where did you get it?'

'From my mother.' The words are out too soon.

She rolls her eyes. 'Yeah. You can always rely on your mother to buy you a jumper.'

The boyfriend is slowly getting to his feet. She takes his arm. I watch them walk away, arm in arm. Powerless.

I am soon on the street, swallowing air that tastes like Chinatown. Lean on a rail beside a pile of black rubbish bags. One of them is torn open, and half-eaten food oozes out like spilt entrails. I brush my nose and there is blood on my fingers. Did I cut myself? I smear the blood between thumb and index, gazes back through the open doors of the club; the woman and her boyfriend come out from the darkness. He skitters, legs escape from beneath him and he clutters through clumsily stacked rubbish bins. The woman titters, helps him to his feet. He hangs from her shoulder, gaping brazenly like a new wound. She brushes me as they walk past.

Four in the morning in my room. Periodically glance out of the window to see if the woman is there, but her window is dark and streaked with the trails of passing cars. I stand by the door.

Begin a slow pace. Walk across the floor. It takes twelve steps to reach the window. Turn, swing on heels, twelve steps to the door and twelve steps back again. Twelve steps. Twelve steps. Twelve steps.

Twelve steps. Twelve steps. I take the woman upon me. Her skin stretched across my brain, her face splayed, distorted, twisted so much it becomes itself again. She's smiling and she sits below me and we've made love and don't move and there are things we can't untie and 'coffee?' and I watch her naked at the sink filling the kettle and placing it to boil and I fold one arm around her stomach and lift up her hair with the other and kiss her neck and she laughs and says 'this is the gift of love' and –

and the annoyed ringing of the telephone.

'H-hello?' I answer.

'Hello. You don't know me, I don't think. My name is Mrs Burroughs. I'm a friend of your mother. I'm sorry to be calling at such an ungodly hour, but your mother insisted. She's been taken rather ill, you see, and insisted you know straight away.'

'What's wrong with her?'

'We doubt it's anything serious. The doctor is due first thing in the morning. It's just that... well, she does worry about you so.'

'Can I talk to her?'

'She's asleep right now, I'm afraid.'

'Well, how about... I'll be round in the morning.'

'Yes, I think she'd like that.'

I kneel on the edge of the bed. Mother's illness is loud in my head. I stub out my cigarette and light another, screw up the empty box and throw it in a corner where I hope it will disappear. And then I turn and see her; a face in the window opposite. The woman is staring straight at me, an empty face.

I gaze into the filthy coffin-coloured river that winds a ruddy path past the back of the house where I was born. Many childhoods spent staring, trying to work out how much the river weighed. Pigeons grouped and chattered on both banks, and I wondered what they found to talk about. Occasionally there were anglers with rods like skyline cranes, who would leave dead fish on the banks or toss the corpses back into the water. The river became for me a river of the dead. I'd imagine I had been borne Moses-like down the river, that my parents had stooped on the muddy bank and pulled my baby body from sodden reeds. This seemed a much more plausible explanation that whispers of fathers who pushed bits of themselves into mothers.

'm in my mother's bedroom and under sunlight the river glistens like
yes. Squares of sun on floor and kingsize bed and sleeping mother.
cent of pine-needles. Blue and green floral bedsheet. The tulips that
pened their petals to me when taken from the garden and shown a
ase of water and a room. A little floral jar filled with coins; I put my
ingers inside, pull out an old five pence piece.

Whenever I think of my
mother I think of tulips
and carnations and roses
and chrysanthemums and
apple blossom; the history
of my mother is a history
of flowers. The bed that
holds her is the one I was
born on, these four blue
walls the first seen by
my womb-stained eyes.

When I arrived she was spread out under the duvet, her eyes lined with
unslept sleep. Mrs Burroughs, sat watching over her, stood to greet
me was I walked in, her face always frozen in the same expression as if
she were a photograph. As I kissed Mother's lemon cheek Mrs
Burroughs bade us farewell.

Mother opens her mouth to speak and I swell within her scent,
gorgeous like a pine forest under snow. I could bathe there for an
eternity, Eden-like and never die.

'How's Lucy?' she says. 'You must bring her to see me again. I hardly
know her. Do you still see Tanya?'

She takes my hands in hers; all those I've loved have similar fragile hands. I shake my head, and she exclaims 'and you were engaged! You seemed so happy with each other.'

A fly skits her pillows. She sighs. 'I'm not well. The doctors say it's serious but I'm not sure. They don't know anything. I know my body.'

She pulls out an envelope filled with photographs of my father, my mother and me. Each photograph is another world. As I turn through them I begin to view my mother in a more human light; she ceases to be a mere soft-handed womb. As she finds sleep I pull out a picture, stare at it for a very long time. My father poses against half of London; the shutter opens and his hilarity is frozen forever. Orange jacket, that jumper too baggy; perhaps he could have combed his hair neater that morning. He is laughing at my mother, and I am unborn.

On the way out I visit the bathroom. Seated on the toilet, staring into the water I can't piss in, air stained with lavender water, bath dry and free of spiders. Above the bath hangs an empty wire washing line.

As a child I stand there gazing at the washing as it dries, in awe at my mother's clothes.

Pull them onto my trembling body, hope that by doing so I won't grow up to be like the men I see around me with anger and penises and pointed fingers.

One day I hear my mother's hand on the door when I'm wearing her turquoise bathrobe; I manage to slam my body against the door before she can open it. 'I'm not wearing any clothes!' I bleat and she goes away, yet I still feel a twinge of excitement at having come so close to discovery. It is thus through my mother that I learn the eroticism of secrets. Nights I lay awake and wish that as puberty consumes me the body I grow into could be female, that I hadn't been sealed within male. Look in the mirror at my thin unclothed body, imagine the slow swell of breasts, that these useless nipples could become fluid, that testicles don't fall to mock me, that blood runs between my legs, that I could carry new life within.

Before I leave the house I stand in the doorway watching mother sleep. The sun shifts shadows across the wall. I walk down to the riverside. Stand gazing at still water. The whole of the world is contained in the river. Ten yards away, an orange-haired woman reads Strindberg. On the river drift flitting gulls and rusted heaps of boats. A boy stands on the far bank with a blue smudge for a tee-shirt. I wish I could tell him what he'll become.

One day when I was a child I fell asleep by the riverside, dreamed my own death. Barely having time to turn before the bullet catches my neck. Topless body coiling and piling itself on the welcome grass. All I know is the pain that is my neck. I roll over, face the sky, birds and sun and bees, want to roll into the water and dissolve amongst the silt and fish, dissolve into my own birth. Cutting the cord and pushing him forward, staring out at the river. The sun a yellow hole in banks of cloud. The wind is dark and supports flurries of rain. In the far distance, giant faceless buildings are being birthed by cranes like gynaecological forceps. Feels like I'm going to be sick. Fingers reek of nicotine. I turn and the orange-haired woman is gone.

Smoke separates us, its source the cigarette in her hand. Slender hands, tiny hands; I pick out their perfections as they trace her body and face. Follow the circles they draw, circles that lead my eyes to hers.

I watched her earlier, as I sat in my room worrying on my mother's behalf. The woman standing at her window, tugging fingers through tangles of hair. She had just showered, and in the last of the sunlight her wet skin was a polished glass ocean undulating between rising points; breasts, shoulders, chin, cheeks, nose. The street below our windows oozes with the tail-end of the rush hour.

As evening descends I hear footsteps in the hall outside. Open the door to a darkened corridor. Suck in the darkness, and in the depths a tiny face. She doesn't need an invitation to enter.

In the half-light my room contains only vague suggestions of furniture beyond the table we sit at. Her body becomes fluid, flows into shadow until it is hard to distinguish one from the other.

When she is close I am weak. Her presence slows me, time is like slurred words, each second vague and difficult to identify. She parts her lips and whispers in a swirl that takes a lifetime.

'Hold on to me... don't be afraid. Close your eyes.' In blind trust I do, and she leans close and kisses the lids.

'Don't say a thing' she breathes. 'I wouldn't believe you, anyway. Words and feelings are all deceits. You should never trust what you hear or feel.'

'I don't even know your name...'

'You don't need to. When we use words we are open to lies. But bodies can never deceive.'

She lights another cigarette and the smoke fills the shadows; the shadows become us, are us, mask the opening up of us. She wears five tiny earrings in one lobe and one earring in the other. Furtive foreplay and soon our bodies are open. Together we slip and slide through a gaping hole in the floor. I try to hold on to the carpet, stop us falling. My nails dig deep. The weight of our bodies and they snap. We fall, together down.

She expands to accommodate me like the jaws of a snake to devour a mouse. I want oblivion in her, trapped inside her belly. Disappear, flow with the blood in her veins.

Linger there, content to exist under her skin. Briefly she becomes me, briefly she is all I am.

Sucked in.

Chewed up.

Swallowed.

Soon regurgitated, flaccid and uncomplaining.

There are times when the idea of meeting someone, removing their clothes and pushing a piece of me inside them seems the most ludicrous thing I could do. But I lie, smothered, just to seem real; imagine filling her, splitting her open, watching her come undone, as if these were the things she'd want me to imagine.

She walks about the room, naked except for Lucy's turquoise bath robe which she has donned. Gathers up her clothes from where they had fallen. Deposits them on the bed. Leaves the room. Piercing silence, then the sound of running water. She re-enters the room, sits by the window, silhouetted by city lights. Her hands touch her face. I wonder how many of her thoughts involve me.

Days pass by under rain, without a sun to light them. I curl up to dreams of my ailing mother, and the darkness edges in around me. That feels good.

Lying on my back, low ceiling above me, door ajar. Old Elton John records through the wall. The woman from the opposite flat has become Lucy. I watch her rise from the bed.

'You're weird' she says.

'Why?'

'Just the way you sit there, always covering yourself up. I don't think I've ever seen you fully clothed in daylight before.'

'But—'

'No, no need for reasons. I don't think I even want to know. I need a shower.'

Slam of bolt on bathroom door. Squeaking rusty tap. Running water. She always insists on showering after we've had sex. I remember making love to Lucy in that same shower. Her back against a wall missing tiles, pears of water hung like tiny Buddhas on her closed eyelids. Lucy and me sat on this bed; she wore black stockings and far too much eye shadow, and

kissed her skin while she shared a dream from the night before. In the dream the two of us are sealed in a room

with walls painted black and I remove her clothes to reveal that she has a penis which she bids me suck and I do and after she has come she pulls me up by the hair and pig-like slits my throat, then slitting her own so that we die together in our own blood.

I know my body as a spindly sequence of blood and bone that gravity pins to the bed. Nerve-endings read out the shape; hip-bone pressed deep, itch at back of neck, curve of side.

I'm only really aware of my body's existence when I can smell it, breathe the sweat that perforates my skin. I can look down, see hands and stomach and penis and legs and feet, but all that looks so superfluous. It's only when my own stench fills these nostrils that I'm pulled inside this body that I feel it as a part of me, not just excess baggage that I drag about beneath myself. It's only when I know my own stink that I become whole.

When the woman re-enters the room, she is wearing Lucy's bathrobe again. 'Does this suit me?' she says, pulling the belt tighter to conceal her slow sagging belly.

'Yeah.'

She stoops, stands over me, hair glistening like a just-born kitten. Towel-dries it, fingers hard into the scalp.

'You're so like my mother...'

She stops towelling. 'Your mother?'

'You have my mother's hands.'

She arches her eyebrows, dumps the towel onto the bed. 'Do you have a cigarette?'

I roll over, rummage through the junk by the side of the bed; pens, scraps of paper, packet of condoms, old keys, matches, hair bands, candles, incense sticks, moisturising lotion, cigarette packet. I flip open the lid; six. Throw the packet at her. She takes one out, lights it, breathes out smoke from between her lips.

'That feels good...' she says, drops the packet on the bed beside the towel.

'Let's talk' I say.

'Why on earth would we want to do that?'

'Because I want to.'

'But what's the point? I told you. Talk only leads to lies.'

She kisses me, seals my lips with hers. I break away. Long silence, pregnant and gaping like a torn Caesarian belly. With words I sew the silence.

'But I don't know anything about you.'

'What do you need to know that could mean anything?'

'I don't know. I don't even know your name.'

'But what's it all got to do with you? You're just a guy I've fucked a few times.'

'Don't tell me then.'

'Once we start to reveal ourselves, we develop ties. Right now we have no hold over each other, and that's the way I want it. If I told you about myself, we'd start to care about each other. I don't want that.'
'You can at least tell me your name.'

'Not even that.'
'But...'
'What?'
'My mother...'
'What?'
'She's dying.'
'Oh.'

Hours pass. She stands, slips out of Lucy's bath robe. Her breasts sway as she squirms into her jeans. I roll over. Dry mouth. She smiles. Her mouth forms 'goodbye', but no words come.

Mother is lying in bed again. Becalmed, her body slowly sinking beneath old grey sheets. The sheets overcoming and becoming her. Every day is a struggle against those sheets. Every day she dies a little more.

Hair the colour of pigeon wings. She takes my hand in hers.
'You won't forget me, will you?' she says.

'Of course not...' I breathe, and she smiles, her eyes heavy with tears that await shedding.

Her hands in mine have the texture of old books. I sigh. The slim hands that have brought my lovers to me are now just frail sacks of bone. Her shrivelled lips parted. Only her eyes betray the stillness. Mother's eyes are a peculiar shade of blue I intuitively know but can never find words for. When I look at her eyes I can't believe she is mortal.

A flicker of day between two nights; light glimmering weakly between two awesome sheets of darkness. The woman is late for the next liaison we have arranged. It's only when I glance at the clock that I realise three hours have passed since the allotted time. I sit in the kitchen deciding what to do and the fridge hums beside me. Look into her flat through the window; drawn curtains. Pick my fingernails. Scratch my itches.

After four hours and the onset of the rush hour I run down the stairs and into the street, into icy drizzle and people moving in all directions and

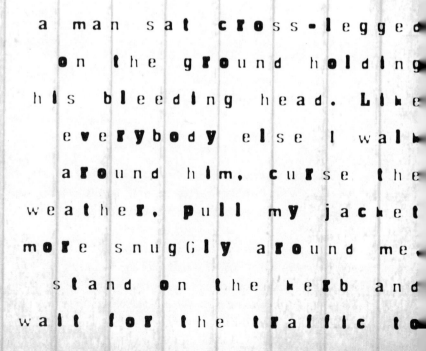

a man sat cross-legged on the ground holding his bleeding head. Like everybody else I walk around him, curse the weather, pull my jacket more snuggly around me, stand on the kerb and wait for the traffic to

change. A squashed-flat
pigeon lies in the
gutter, looks like a
textbook illustration
of a pigeon's insides.

The woman's door is ajar. I knock. Silence but for rain and wind. I
:k the door; it shrieks and swings open.

A small hallway. Broken chairs, table, scraps of wood, paper, glass.
other door ajar in the opposite wall. I walk over and push it open,
ass crunching like bones beneath my feet.

A bedroom. Sheetless mattress, black walls, window, bare
orboards, box of matches, piles of clothes. The woman is lying on an
ormous cushion in the corner, robe a shroud around her; the body
neath it is a tapestry of bruises. Her arms twitch as she clutches the
emory of me. I bend, take her in my arms. Her mouth falls open. A
il of blood runs from her lip.

I want to cry.

'You look so innocent...' she says.

She shivers, and I pull her closer. Kiss her hair, feel hot tears
om my eyes. One of her earrings has been pulled out, and the lobe
eps blood.

She sits. 'I want you to go. I want to be alone.'

'Talk to me...' I pull her robe tighter around her, fasten the buttons
ross her chest, wipe the blood from her mouth.

'I have nothing to say to you.'

She stands, looks down at me; a sound behind us.

'What's that?' I ask.

'Look if you must. Then go. Please. I need a cigarette. I need a
ower.'

She reaches for Marlboros, shaking as she lights one. My vision
zes in and out; for a moment all I know is a red blur as she lifts the
cket. I walk across the room. Open the door.

The room contains two bodies; one male and one female. They
n't register me at all. The woman favours the shuttered window.

She stands there naked, cradles breasts in her arms. Thick wedge of brown hair becoming blonde as she steps from the shadow. The man sits alone and stares at the floor. A ring through each nipple. He is sticking needles under his fingernails, seeing how much pain he can endure. Flinches, winces, screws up eyes; withdraws the needles then pushes them in again.

The woman touches his body. He gazes at her treble clef earrings; two front teeth stick out over his top lip. They laugh and punch each other.

'I think I've just burst something' she says, and they laugh louder.

She straddles him, takes him inside her and they become one skin. I watch their writhing awhile. Turn away, stare at a poster on the wall above them. White on red bordered by yellow; white birds –parrots, maybe, or cockatiels –on a branch, surrounded by crimson flowers. Mustard strip down each side. Gaudy curtains.

He rises from the floor. Penis still half-hard, thick as a wrist and glistening like liver. He looks up at me, barks out a laugh.

'Enjoy the show?' he drawls, walks past me and through the open door I came in by. I stare at the woman lying on the floor. She takes a tissue from a box by the window, dabs it between her legs. Returns my stare then looks at the sodden tissue, tosses it aside, replaces it with another. Turquoise evening. Stacks of paperbacks with water-warped covers. Yesterday's crumpled Evening Standard.

Night has come and gone outside. I stare at the telephone. My mouth is stale. I dial mother's number, count thirty five rings before hanging up. Fret my way to the kitchen. Sort through the pile of cups and plates in the sink, pull out the cleanest glass. Rinse it, fill it with water. As I drink I hear the telephone, am there within three rings.

'Hello?'

'It's Lucy...'

'How are you?' Her voice makes me want to cry.

'I'm okay.'

'Your father?'

'Huh? Getting better. Hey listen, I'm on my way home.'

'When?'

'Guess I'll be home tomorrow. Late afternoon. Maybe even evening.'

'Great. I've missed you.'

'Yeah. Missed you as well. What have you been doing?'

'Getting by. My mother is ill.'

'Serious?'

'Yeah. I think she might die.'

'Oh, I'm sure it won't come to that.'

'I want to be with her. She asked about you.'

'Well I get back tomorrow. We'll go and see her together.'

'I'd like that very much.'

'Listen, I have to go because I'm in a call box and I'm all out of change. I'll see you tomorrow.'

'Yeah. Bye.'

I dial my mother's number again. No reply. Perhaps I should go d see her. Strange that she's not answering. Even stranger than the ring in Lucy's voice.

The doorbell startles me. It is the woman from across the road. She iles. 'Hi.'

'Hi.'

'Aren't you going to invite me in?'

I step aside. She walks into the lounge. 'I'm sorry you had to see like that yesterday' she says. 'I didn't want you to.'

'Do you want to talk about it?'

'Not much.'

'That woman. Who was she?'

'She's not important. Just a woman. She doesn't matter.'

'I hated seeing you like that. I care about you.'

'Don't say that.'

'But it's true.'

'Don't say it!' She walks away from me.

'Lucy's coming home soon.'

'Who?'

'Lucy. The woman I live with.'

'Oh.' She raises her arm. A line of light on bruised pale skin. Hands er her mouth.

'What'll happen to us then?'

'Guess we'll just stop. You won't need me anymore.'

'But...'

'But what?'

'I don't know.' I stand by the window. Dead flies are gathered on the window ledge.

'Want one last fuck?' Isabelle says.

'I couldn't stand it.'

'Why?'

'All that pain.'

'It's nothing. Do you want to fuck or not?'

She walks towards me, slips off her shirt, naked underneath. She has a scar above her left nipple I've never noticed before.

'A drunk ex-lover's cigarette...' she says as she starts to undo my buttons.

'What are you doing?' I ask.

'What do you think? Undressing you.'

I pull away from her.

'What's up with you?'

'I don't like being naked?'

'Why? Think you're any different to anybody else?'

'No.'

'So why is it?'

I turn away from her. 'Something. Because... I love you.'

'Do you?'

'Yes...'

'So what do you want to say?'

'I'm eighteen. It's my birthday. I visit a friend. I first met him two years before; that was on my birthday, as well. He makes coffee, wishes me happy birthday and happy anniversary of our friendship. 'I've got a present for you' he says, holds a gift out. I stare at the plain blue wrapping.

Little red bow. Unwrap it; a book of William Blake poems. I thank him. 'Come here' he says. I pause, and he says 'you're beautiful. I love you.' 'No you don't, I say, it's just lust.'

He shrugs. 'Lust, love, come here anyway.'

He pulls off his shirt, walks towards me, embraces me. 'Hold me' he says. My hands hang lose around his waist. He says 'No, like you mean it.' I tighten a little; his back is covered with hairs, feels rough compared to the smooth female bodies I'm used to. 'You're beautiful...' he repeats over and over. 'I can't help wanting somebody as beautiful as you.' He takes roses from a vase on the table; pushes them, one by one and still dripping water, through my hair. Dots my

eck with kisses, his stubble coarse against my skin. I drop my arms
nd look at the door. 'What's the matter?' he asks. I don't reply. 'Tell
e' he says. 'Tell me what you want me to do with you.' 'But you won't
o what I want you to do' I answer, as he begins to undo the buttons
own the front of my shirt. I push his hands away; he puts them
ack again. 'What's do you want?' he asks. 'For you to leave me alone.'
ut I can't. I want you. I think you want to, as well, you just won't admit it
yourself. I'll pay you to be with me. How much do you want?' He takes
ut his wallet, throws a pile of bank notes on the table. 'That enough?
ore?' 'I don't want it' I say. And he strokes my hair, telling me over and
ver that no one's ever made him feel like I do. I say 'no' but he won't
sten, tries to pull my shirt off; I struggle and he gives up, goes off to piss.
curl up into a foetus in the corner of the sofa. When he comes back he
ills off my clothes, lifting limbs when needs be. I resist at first but know
won't make any difference. I hate my body because he wants it, the body
pins beneath him. The rest I only remember in flashes.

The way he traces his
half-hard dick against my
thigh, leaves a trail of
come. His hands and mouth
and dick and body on me.
How he gets pissed off
when I don't have a hard-
on. Trying to push his
dick into my mouth, or
trying to get inside me.

uck it' he says. No. Pools of clothing on the floor. The sun is on the
oor with them. Two walls of books look down at us. I want to be ugly,

destroyed, non-existent. He sits next to me and wanks. 'Give my your hand' he says; I don't, he takes it and puts it on his dick, puts his on too. 'Oh, I'm gonna come...' he says. I close my eyes; when I open them again all I see are trails of semen. The flowers have fallen from my hair and now lie squashed on the floor. I curl up and cry. Then the phone rings.'

'Why did you tell me about that?' she says.

'I love you.'

'Don't say that.'

'Why?'

'Because you don't. It's just sex.'

'No.'

'Look...' Her nostrils flare wider. 'I don't want to be cruel to you. I don't want to hurt you. But you don't love me. You need me. Perhaps you desire me. But I doubt that. The last thing you do is love me. It's just need. You need me because you don't like yourself. It's not me. Anyone will do. Anyone who can protect you, who won't leave you alone, because when you're alone you have to look at yourself. And when you do you hate what you see. You don't love me. You don't even know what love is. I have to go.'

She leaves the room. Clicks door quietly shut. I take a cracked glass in my fingers, run the edge along my skin.

Alone again. I can't sleep with anticipation at Lucy's return. Can't wait to feel her skin, push back her hair with fingers hard on her scalp, tast and breathe her scent. I imagine keys in locks that are never her.

Perhaps I should call my mother. I watch the dark city laze before me. The flat across the street is dark and empty. A clear night sky above me. I shake into sleep.

I wake to the sound of sirens. Open the window. Lean out. A police car and an ambulance bathed n swirling red light.

Two men carry a

stretcher out of the

building opposite and

into the ambulance.

Police mill in all directions, their movements slow and clothes dark. The woman's light is on. Police in her room. In the street two policemen hold the woman's lover between them.

The telephone rings beside me. 'Hello?'

'Hello. This is Mrs Burroughs.'

'Yes?'

'Well, I'm afraid... it's your mother. She passed away in her sleep...'

I drop the receiver. My head out of the window. Rain on me. A thousand years of futile words splash from my body with the rain into the street.

I am curled up crying on the floor when Lucy's key unlocks the door. I look up; through tear-red eyes she enters the room. Her jacket is flecked with rain. Her mouth opens wider. She drops her bag by the door. Whispers my name, tongue between lips; takes me in her arms.

'Mother's dead...' I whisper.

Our eyes meet. There's nothing else to say. We sit there for hours, me coiled up in her. The only sound her heartbeat against my head. Words no longer matter.

'Do you want to get into bed?' Lucy asks as twilight edges into the room. 'No sex. Just hugs.'

I smile at the impending darkness, nod. 'Were you waiting for night before you asked me?'

'Yeah. I know how much you like the shadows.'

She leads me by the hand to the bedroom. I sit on the bed, watchas she slips off her jacket, walks over to the wardrobe. Clatter of coat hangers as she sorts through the clothes hanging there.

'Where's my blue robe?' she asks.

' A woman got killed here.'

'The clatter stops. 'What do you mean, here?'

I sit in my hands. 'In the flat across the street.'

Fifteen seconds. Lucy's mouth open but no words. Then 'It happens. Do you know where my robe has gone?'

My fingers draw circles on the street. 'No. You don't understand. A woman was killed. I knew her.'

'Did you kill her?'

'Of course not.'

'Then what difference does it make?'

She closes the wardrobe, walks over to me. My head on her stomach. Her careful hands in my hair. 'I lied to you' she says.

'About what?'

'My father. He was ill, but that's not the reason I went away.'

'Then why?'

'I was pregnant. Your child.'

'Mine?'

'Don't look at me like that. Of course it was yours.'

I stand by the wall. 'But I thought you slept with other people.'

'Yeah, but I always made them use condoms. You're the only one I trust enough to let come inside me. I know you're faithful.'

'So what happened?'

'When I left here I didn't know what to do. I thought about abortion. I'd had one before, sure, but this was different. You know, that last time, I didn't even feel like I was pregnant? This time I had this constant sensation inside me. I'd wake up sometimes and it would hurt and I'd claw the walls and scream. But I cared. I'd never really thought about that before, could feel it inside me, in my stomach, in my heart, in my blood. Abortion would have been easy, a way of evading the pain of a piece of us. I couldn't. Not this time. Then I lost it. Miscarriage.'

Her eyes shine with flecks of light. 'You want to talk about your mother?' she asks.

'So much death. Seems like I surround myself with it.'

'Tell me. Talk to me. I never knew I wanted you. Needed that pain. Needed it to tell me I wanted you. Needed that power. When did you last eat?'

'Can't remember. didn't think about food that much.'
'I'll fix us something.'

I watch as she leaves the room. Maybe later we'll make love. I stand
in the shadows and wait for her. Find me a place where I'll never been
een, shadows and the shell of Lucy. She comes back into the room,
ack into my arms. Touches my head.

'We'll be fine together...'
Her fingertips on beads
of sweat, then to my
eyes, my lips.
'We'll be fine. We have
each other. This is the
gift of love.'

standfirm do not paperout clock-in walk out under bricks and bottles and cans full of sand dancing on bus shelters and police vans a man in a black mask stares silently and intently at the cops *scum scum scum* José falls in love *DON'T RUN* dry throat smoking a spliff the texture of riot shields the sinis headlights do you have to ella no lla no pasaran *1,2,3,4 we don't want y fucking law* dance is human nat human protest the police lining up Piccadilly one has his truncheon out mate Tom says he must be pissi

Paul Montigue

mself say summit mister inner
asefire stroking the white horse
tract claws *Fuck Off Fuck Off Fuck Off*
archlights clambering over railings in
e dark the way of conspiracy fake ex-
ell's Angel and his mother lover
umbling out of the bar donde esta la
belleza donde esta ella
crude

thoughts insomniac caressing feeling
for a moment of energy *don't run* there
is no reason to this *they're losing.*

AUSE

Guided by unconsciousness.
La rubia, la rubia. Le gusto a
ella. To start. I wake up and
perform the ritual of staring
vacantly at the ceiling letting the
sleep drain from my eyes and
invoking the remnants of bizarre
fantasies. Throwing back the purple
duvet I reach for the corner of a bath
robe protruding from under a pile of
books, paper, cassettes and plastic
bags. In the bathroom I run a bath.
Splat! Splat! Splat! gets some of the
fast departing roaches except the
clever big bastard one who drops off
the wall. Someone told me I should
burn them as when they die they
drop their eggs but I feel pretty
stupid chasing them with 3 for £1
lighters. My thoughts drift to the
council kicking in doors and
putting Sitex over them. Clean
teeth, get dressed, toast and
Marmite, toast and honey,
flamenco music, to work. It
drizzles shredded wheat style
into sparkling waters of heavy

tred   the
rning wood smash-
g up concrete slabs
ake sense of these last
v days *Kill the Bill, Kill the*
I, Kill the Criminal Justice Bill
w heavy cannot hold in this
ger it's winter it's freezing
u feel like shit and you're
rring paint with your hands
e banners Class War Charter 88
sbian Avengers collective view
nning the war over the roaches
alant in hair pointing the gun
ere the hell are we no pasaran
nigos   see   them   crawling

101

islands the bass in my ears the road drill feet to the right across Kennington
Road dodging the heavy traffic this long walk bursting
pride and snatches of glory past Lambeth Walk
and into view the slimy Thames. I am no longer
awake. Febrile thoughts race through my mind. A ella no le
gusta. Bricks and bottles. Mounted police charging through
park. I sit here now isolated and stunned. They know
something is wrong.

the rage subsides turn away sent
cunning eviction notices by the council
some Spanish geezer returns Tom's
crowbars when R and his gang
come round to our squat they're
buying tobacco in France do you want hashish
Elmore James Public Enemy Loop Guru the kids
laugh speak mister those explosions are deep
within it's OK to blame the parents RAGE the man standing
at the bar drinking too fast he couldn't even chat anyone up on
speed so ANGER a la theecotico amigo no dragon no butterfly no
tiger just mouse an apathetic swipe at the roaches yeah no tiger
just Blair rabbit rabbit rabbit sedentary lives just hermits in flats
SAY IT but the villagers they are all one

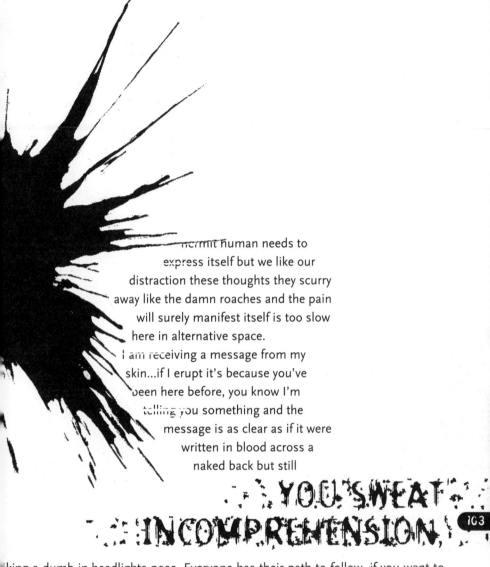

hermit human needs to
express itself but we like our
distraction these thoughts they scurry
away like the damn roaches and the pain
will surely manifest itself is too slow
here in alternative space.
I am receiving a message from my
skin...if I erupt it's because you've
been here before, you know I'm
telling you something and the
message is as clear as if it were
written in blood across a
naked back but still

YOU SWEAT
INCOMPREHENSION,

king a dumb in-headlights pose. Everyone has their path to follow, if you want to
dge through the mud that's your choice. It could be so peaceful but this never
rsts in public it's like a mausoleum in this room soon someone will enter and
rt measuring you up.
e end of a savage week in this junk city. It's 4am and I'm looking out of my 5th
or window, past the silent, brooding tower blocks, towards Big Ben and the
uses of Parliament. A cockroach crawls along the ledge above the heating duct,
t I have no urge to kill it. I think I'll make myself some symbolic tea.

EVERyTHING THeRe IS ABOUT AN

BY MATHEW PITT

Oi, this morning right— Jesus. Rock gear. Straight off the boat this stuff. Red seal. Got it off Lenny didn't I? I tell you, Lenny, he's fucked up. Other day right, he says to me 'Yesterday I saw a dead crow in the middle of the road...and it's Jimmy Hendrix.' I mean what the fuck's that supposed to mean? He's fucked up is what I'm saying. Them Es innit? I tell you, bit of puff every now and then fair enough right, but them disco bisuits, they'll mess with your head. Yeah? All chemicals and stuff innit? I mean you don't know what's in it, is what I'm saying. But he's alright, Lenny.

Yeah. This morning. I'm walking down Electric Avenue. Right? About eleven o'clock this is, 'cos I've just signed on haven't I? So I'm walking along and I tell you it's mad down there. Everyone shouting and pushing and geezers wheeling about them little dump-trolleys. And music playing. Stinks too, I tell you. All them bins full of fishheads and rotting veg and stuff.

So. Yeah. I'm getting kind of uptight, yeah? 'Cos I'm in a hurry and I wanna get home.

WhoAh!

I'm out of it, I tell you. That's wha mean, see? Twenty quid. Red seal. Y go down the Bricklayers they'll ask y twenty-five for a fucking liquorice allso That's what I mean. Lenny. He's alrigh So I'm walking along and —tell the tru —I dunno why I'm in such a hurry mean I'm on the dole right? I nev used to be. I tell you I've had more fu ing jobs than I do not know wha Serious. But now I'm unemployed such aren't I? So what am I gonna do day? Sit on me bum and watch the fu ing telly, that's what. And stare at n ants. I swear, I got this glass tank in n

rious. About five hundred of the little ggers. That's a colony, innit? I tell u, I'm not being funny or nothing but ey are amazing creatures, ants are. me people think ants are stupid, but ey aint you know. The way they orga- ze themselves and all work together. I l you I can sit and watch them for urs. I used to work in a laboratory, e? Security guard. That's how I got erested. Anyway. Yeah. There's this ezer in front of me, yeah? Jesus. I'm ving fucking palpitations here.

d bloke. I can't see his face right, but 's got grey hair and he's kind of oped over yeah? And the skin on the ck of his neck is all sort of thick and inkled. And he's carrying a table on head. Serious. Well, I'm thinking get nove ongrandad, 'cos he's going like mile a fucking fortnight yeah, and he's ing my head in. So. Well. I push past n, don't I? I don't mean nothing by it, ust wanna get home. Yeah? Well, he s over, don't he? Aaargh! he goes— ops the fucking table he's carrying, s arse over tit. Well, fair enough, he's old geezer right so I'm sort of ncerned, yeah? So I bends wn to pick him up. And ddenly I'm thinking – fuck! ere's this look on his face. Right?

He's holding his arm and he's kind of shivering and gasping for breath. Yeah? Well. He's only having a bleeding heart-attack. Hang about. Fuck. I tell you, I can't roll these things to save my life. You wanna see Lenny. It's like hey presto, Paul fucking Daniels. I like that, seeing something done proper. Used to work in this bottling factory, didn't I? I swear, there's this geezer there could roll 'em one handed. Serious. I mean it's only rolling a joint, I know that, but you gotta repect them for it what I'm saying.

Yeah.

Well. Next thing I know this lady's trying to lift the poor geezer up. She's like posh, yeah? Headscarf and little quilted jacket and rings on her fingers. She's got her hands in the geezer's armpits right and she's trying to pull him up. Well. I tell you, one thing you should never do if someone has a heart-attack, is you should never move them about. I used to be a lifeguard in a swimming pool right, so that's how I know. I know what I'm saying, is what I'm saying.

Rock gear.

So I tell her 'Leave him alone. Jesus Christ. You'll probably fucking kill him.' And she looks up at me all sort of snooty yeah? And she puts the geezer down again. She knows I'm right, right, but she don't like being told what to do by some feller what's got tattoos on his fingers. Yeah?

Right. Next thing– I'm not being funny, this is a true fucking story– this other geezer, he goes 'Anything I can do?' He's about twenty I reckon. Suede jacket. Long hair. Converse boots. And he's carrying this little plastic bag with a couple of videos in it. I'm serious. *Anything I can do?* Typical fucking student. I mean I'm not saying anything against education or nothing.– I used to work as a porter at South Bank poly, and some of them students they're alright, yeah?– but what I mean is I pay my taxes so as they can sit on their arses and read faggotty books for three years and what fucking good does it do? I mean fair enough, the geezer's trying to help, thousands wouldn't,

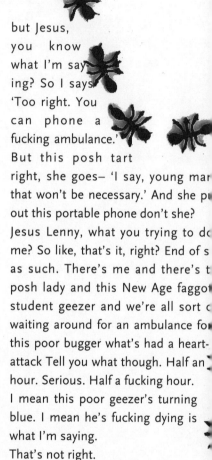

but Jesus, you know what I'm saying? So I says 'Too right. You can phone a fucking ambulance.' But this posh tart right, she goes– 'I say, young man that won't be necessary.' And she p[u] out this portable phone don't she? Jesus Lenny, what you trying to d[o] me? So like, that's it, right? End of s[tory] as such. There's me and there's t[he] posh lady and this New Age faggo[t] student geezer and we're all sort [of] waiting around for an ambulance fo[r] this poor bugger what's had a heart-attack Tell you what though. Half an hour. Serious. Half a fucking hour. I mean this poor geezer's turning blue. I mean he's fucking dying is what I'm saying.

That's not right.

That's the government, that is. **Yeah.**

But what I'm saying– I'm not being funny or nothing– is like now, after the event as such, I'm thinking– I know I'm fucking stoned and everything– but I'm thinking what's that kid got in the bag? Them videos. What's he gonna watch? Arnie? Cindy Crawford? Some intellectual bollocks with subtitles and stuff? Know what I'm saying? I mean I won't never know, is whatI'm saying. And that posh tart. What's she doing walkindown Electric Avenue eleven o'clock in the morning? And like she probably thinks I'm some sort of fucking criminal 'cos of the way I talk and I've got tattoos on my fingers. Bet she'd never guess I know like fucking everything there is about ants. First impressions as such, innit?
Wonder how that old geezer is

they put him in the ambulance.
Shakes you up. Death innit? But there you go see? Another case in point. As such. I'm thinking like– what's the daft bugger doing carrying a table on his head?

Know what I'm Saying?

Jesus.

CARCASS

by Lorna G Ruskin

Here today, gone tomorrow. Friends.
Incongruous, immortal we are. Ha ha ha. You can't trust them. A
don't you just love them. Friends.

Fleshly pink.

Fleshly your favourite word, for the moment. Fleshly plink, you
slurred at the last party, dropping another one into my glass.
Giggling, eyelashes fluttering. Plink plink fizz.

Friends.

We draw one another, cheaper than life classes. More of a laugh,
ha ha ha. Plink plink fizz.

You draw me like some fat, child's pig. Round. And colour me in
with felt pen. Useless at art. You and me both. But try not to go
over the lines.

Lines on my face, hands and feet. Belly lines.

Neck lines, boundary lines. White lines on my thighs. Please don'

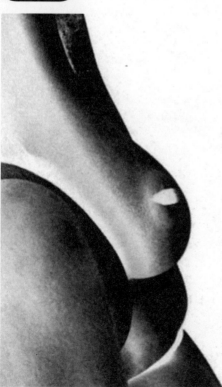

cross them.

Like a child's drawing of pigs, fleshly pink. You and me both.

In summertime we stretched ourselves out in the back yard. Together we lived by the gates of the abattoir, in a square, red brick house, on a flat, bare industrial estate, south of the town. Burly truck drivers leered over the fence from their cabs, truck backs filled with black cows, meat on last legs.

Meat on slabs, concrete slabs, we turned on our too-thin white towels, belly-pink. Pink bellies to the sun, burnt under lines of white washing hung shimmering in the blue air. The air had a smell to it, flies buzzed in it, searching.

Flesh.

'Hair today, gone tomorrow.'

We pick up our Immac in tubes from Superdrug, carry it off with smug faces, linked arms, and pits full of condemned black fuzz.

The first time we were had. Mine was the bed, yours was the floor. Carpet burns. We turned our heads to watch one another, mounted and pierced. Craning our necks,

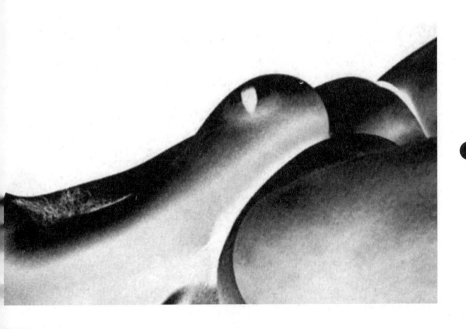

rolling our eyes. The beasts were triumphant, bare back riding, rumps bare and bouncing, beautiful, bouncing.

Impale, impale. Close your eyes and impale.

Back in the yard again, under the sun in our sun-filled back yard. Fenced in, boxed. Penned in square garden of concrete. Our backs the sky, an arc of pure blue.

Trucks driven past the creosote fence, drivers gawping. Thick, suntanned arms sporting tattooed love ladies and checked shirts. Blue denim crotches, shifting in their seats. Hot and itching.

We lay topless in bikini bottoms, laughing. Lemonade sipping through candy striped straws. Rolling over, a freak breeze stirred ou nipples.

Til the day when they broke through the fence. Grunting and snorting, snorting, grunting. Nostrils flared, tossing their fine head spraying saliva and stamping their hooves. Into our space.

Impale, impale. On our backs, impale. Captured forever, and pinne

Into our space.

Legs smoo
and hair fre
scissor wid
in the air,

which feels cold. Summer outside. Boxed in a cold room at the back of the house.

Impale, impale.

Wrap your pink legs round his strong ox's back, sweetheart run your soft fingertips over his hide.

Humping, humping.

We turn our heads to watch one another. His sweat drips onto your face. Brown locks, thick curled, red neck straining. Eyes closed.

Impale, impale.

We reach out to touch one another, arms outstretched, hands open, fingers reaching. Eyes pleading. Grasping nothing but air.

I long for your touch.

Mine is blond and red faced from pumping. Pure gasoline. Set me on fire, if you can, honey, while I stare at t sky beyond virginal nets, white and lifelessly hung at the window.

Til the day when they broke through the fence. Grunting and snorting, snorting, grunting. Nostrils flared, tossing their fine heads, spraying saliva and stamping their hooves.

t a nod, at a wink, we throw
ack our arms, you and me.
rch our bodies, and squeal.
oth of us, little pigs, synch-
onised pink.

haken from dumb animal
ode, they fight to stay
ounted, joined to us where
e only black fuzz we have
ft disappears over a mound.
pen their eyes to watch
ur spectacular display. and
ollapse, heavy on our ribs, as
ubdued, we subside. Bury
eir noses in sweet
melling, fuzz free pits.
uzzle nuzzle. Sleep
eking.

heir pistols are spent.I look
own at you lying there on
e floor, weighted, limbs
played, as if he had fallen on
ou from a great
eight.

ater, I call you a slag.
e stand, hands on hips,
d faced and shouting. While
utside smoke rises
om the abattoir's chimney,
nother batch down. And
gnorant of our angry
ces and the cruel words we
ill come to regret,
e smoke rises, rising
erenely into the calm,
lear blue sky, rising beyond
e back yard with its careful
ne of white washed sheets.

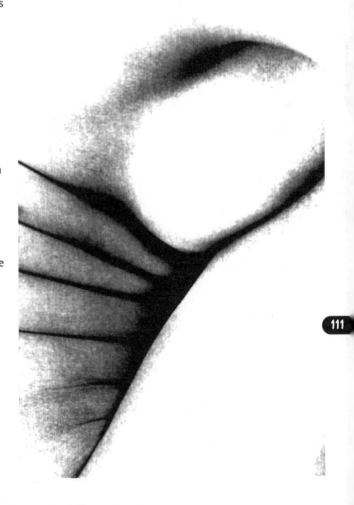

He stood on the pavement, staring down at his battered trainers. The autumn leaves swirling in wind-blown eddies spiralled past, and he looked about, searching for the cause of their particular movement. He found it in the form of an alcove in the building behind, which captured the wind's force and turned it back on itself by the close arrangement of walls, before sending it off in a twist of the season's detritus. His gaze fell to his trainers once more. He checked his watch.

The car accelerated as it exited right from Mile Lane, and was nudging almost twice the speed limit by the time it passed The Coach & Horses. She was late. The road was quiet and empty under the darkening sky, and the roar of the vehicle's engine was her only company. She glanced at the faintly glowing green figures of the car's clock, and made a mental note to correct its time. She hadn't yet put it back an hour.

The streetlight beside him hummed as it flared into life. A little late he thought, as he looked up at the night's first stars. It's at this time of day, he remembered someone once telling him, that you can sometimes see the sun and the moon in the sky together. He looked about, but could see neither.

Her fingers, drumming along to an imaginary tune beating against the steering wheel, prompted her to switch on the radio, but static and white noise was all that greeted her. She frowned and jabbed at the 'off' button. With the needle approaching ninety, the Harps Road intersection went by in a blur.

He checked his watch again. The watch she gave him, and he cursed her half-heartedly under his breath. Glancing up the road, where the trees overhung the corner, a small glittering caught his eye. He paused, and then wrapping his jacket more tightly about him, started up the road. Along the way he turned the collar up on his coat, and reached into his pocket, fingers feeling for the 'play' button on his Walkman. He found it, and turned up the volume.

Reaching the corner, he stooped to examine the object that had glittered and caught his attention. A damaged cats-eye torn from its rubber surround and slightly displaced from the centre of the road.

112

The car slowed into the corner and began to accelerate out, as he began to stand, the broken cats-eye in his hand. She screamed as the figure suddenly reared up in front of the car. She slammed on the brakes and simultaneously slammed into him. Stopping distances were all she could think of.

The car appeared from nowhere, silent under the sound of the Walkman, and took him in the thighs. The impact lifting him onto the vehicle's bonnet and sending the cats-eye hurtling into the air. His face met with the toughened glass of the windscreen and shattered it, before momentum took hold and sent his body over the car's roof and onto the cold tarmac behind. The cats-eye landed with a bounce.

She forced the car into an abrupt stop at a hedgerow and, pumped with adrenalin, was out of it and running up the road in an instant. As she recognised his jacket,

her movement became dysfunctional. His fallen body was dark on dark; against the road's hard surface, against the background of trees and night sky. The corner of his jacket flapped in the wind, and she fell to her knees by his body. It started to rain.

Just under the sound of the wind, she could make out the beat of his Walkman. And somewhere to her left, a displaced cats-eye spun awkwardly in the road, slowing to a halt.

PAUL HAMLYN

STORM

We needed a storm to calm us down after those burning evenings. But not this one, this was hers, she'd called it while we thrashed together on the narrow bed.

She stood naked at the window of the flat, staring out wide-eyed, warm and sticky. Her aura bent the space around her, drawing in dust and small insects. She slapped at a mosquito, crushed it on the killing field of her thigh. I watched her deep shadows searched out by lightning, glowing blue, supernatural and obscene. There was a bus-stop in the street below. People huddled beneath the shelter. See another world if they glanced upwards. But they wouldn't, would they?

She giggled at the flashes, knowing they were meant for her, a salute or a warning. Rough magic spat out, conjured by the thump of flesh on flesh. She turned back to the bed and hauled me up. Flung on a trenchcoat several sizes too big, nothing else. We're going out, she said. I knew bet-

ter than to argue. I pulled on jeans and a torn cagoule. The rain was crazy.

The streets were blurred, tarmac was a steaming three-phase no-man's-land. Car headlights blinked against the deluge. She grinned at the people in the bus queue. Silly sheep waiting for deliverance in a red tin box. She would go out and grab it. Sirens blared. Dogs barked at her rampaging pheromones.

A fire engine swerved round the corner and the tide roared in, drenching feet, licking a shop windows. Another one behind. A convoy. Come on, she said, dragged me with her as she ran, following the wail and the beacon of the brake-lights. We jumped on to the tailboard, bare feet squeezing out a purchase, hands clinging to the coiled hose as a waterfall ran off the ladder.

My arms snaked around her waist, felt her soft heat through the fabric, slid inside. Contours of her meaty arse picked out by the dampness, nestling against me. We kissed, the vehicle lurched over a bump in the road. Tongues were bitten, just an accident. We laughed. This could catch on.

Did people notice us? They tried not to. Just a prank, no point in getting worked up about it. Enough to worry about already, just getting home in this. But some knew. Knew there was another story, and they weren't in it. Kept off our fast-track, wandering among the sidings.

Hard to say how long we'd been driving. Smell of smoke from somewhere close. Sickly, sputtering, flogged into combustion. The rain was slackening, the night was close as a second skin. We looked ahead, peering along the flanks, and saw the glowing buildings. Warehouse complex on a small trading estate.

The fire engine pulled into the forecourt, men jumped out. We jumped too, landed in muddy water and ran back to the road. If they'd seen us, they were too busy to bother giving out grief. We stood under a tree, watching the men uncoil the hose. Two other engines already at work. Plastic packaging, I said. Tell by the black smoke. It'll take some putting out. Wonder what started it. Lightning, she said. Her spell reaching out its tentacles. She grinned.

They were holding it at bay. The rain had almost stopped now.

BUT THEN A LOUD BANG,

I staggered back across the yard, she ran ahead. Came to a low wall, climbed over on to damp grass. Beyond, a chain-link fence and a field of astroturf. The sports ground I set down the stash and she tore it open, strong arms cruel with the cardboard,

and dragon's breath from the warehouse next door, a metal shutter peeled back. She nudged my arm, pointed to the signboard glowing faintly in the flames. Distributors of Wines and Spirits. I feel a thirst coming on, she said. She gave me her look again. She'd forgive me if I refused to go along with her, but she knew I couldn't.

We crept round the back, found a window, cracked from the heat. You're not serious, I said. Wait a minute, she said, and kissed me gently. The fire belched inside the building and a door fell open. Look, she said, we're in luck. A pallet leaned wearily against the jamb. Stacked with boxes of malt whisky, no wonder it looked half-cut. She ran over, hauled one off the top and shoved it at my midriff. Now I was an accomplice, willing or not.

hauling out a bottle, slightly warm. She unscrewed, slugged, and wiped her lips. I hesitated, looked at her and grabbed another. Cheers, I said.

Back in the yard the building wobbled, flared, and melted with a hot gust. We saved these, she said, patting the box. We were just in time. She swigged again, lay back and pulled me down to her. The ground was a quagmire, the sky glowing, thunder still rumbling in the distance.

I pulled the coat open, ran my hand over her plump belly, strong centre of her. Felt her breath deepen as my fingers set off on new footpaths. She grunted and rolled on top of me, smiled as her breasts draped across my face. My back was soaking, crazy place for a shag, trust her to choose it. Still, might as well enjoy. By the way, she said, something to say before we start. I'm leaving you tomorrow.

BRIGITTE

by Sarah Jane

The Key is
turned. Extend
yourself-
it is the Nile,
the sun is shining
every-
where you turn is
luck.

Louise Gluck

BARDOT

ummer heat's so nagging it's piss-asy to incite nightmares. You toss nd turn, strip sheets and clothes, nd still you writhe in your own kin. Too tired to talk or eat, even reaming feels uncomfortable, espe-ially when woken by insects. umble sex, like eating chilli in a ornado; furious and unfamiliar. Vell, winter's just the same, only ss good-byes, and the other end f the scale; too damn cold to uck, and too freezing to sleep, specially in this apartment. Veather's schizophrenic, you either sweat or perish, there's no in-between, no alternative. Today was weird.

I've been thinking more than usual, which is never a good sign. I've been thinking about Jane and about Aimee and Travis, and one minute I'm happy, and then I'm in tears, missing every-body like crazy. I blame it on the sky, so clear and so damn blue, the kind of blue you used to dye your hair. Electric, neon, way-out, the kind of blue your folks would really hate.

I went out walking earlier, and the ground was mighty hard, the grass crisp. It was lovely, frosty and clear, but hiding layers of thick ice, so I kept almost slipping on my ass, but never quite making it, never actually

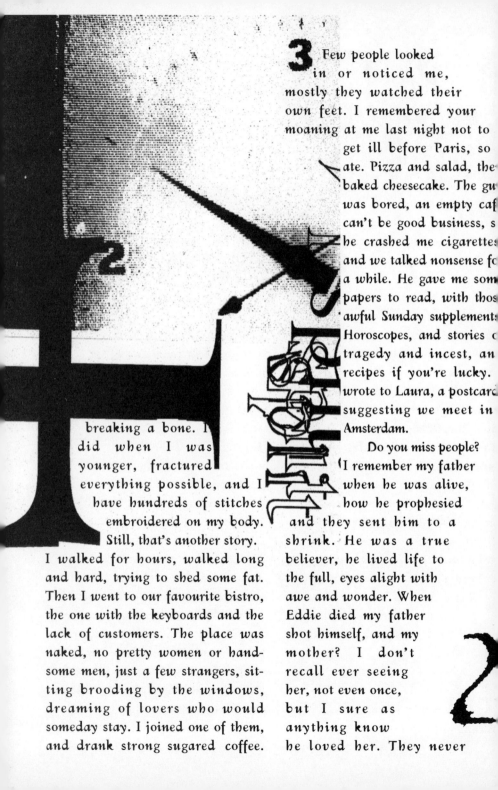

3 Few people looked in or noticed me, mostly they watched their own feet. I remembered your moaning at me last night not to get ill before Paris, so ate. Pizza and salad, the baked cheesecake. The gu was bored, an empty caf can't be good business, s he crashed me cigarettes and we talked nonsense fo a while. He gave me som papers to read, with thos awful Sunday supplements Horoscopes, and stories c tragedy and incest, an recipes if you're lucky. wrote to Laura, a postcarc suggesting we meet in Amsterdam.

Do you miss people? I remember my father when he was alive, how he prophesied and they sent him to a shrink. He was a true believer, he lived life to the full, eyes alight with awe and wonder. When Eddie died my father shot himself, and my mother? I don't recall ever seeing her, not even once, but I sure as anything know he loved her. They never

breaking a bone. I did when I was younger, fractured everything possible, and I have hundreds of stitches embroidered on my body. Still, that's another story. I walked for hours, walked long and hard, trying to shed some fat. Then I went to our favourite bistro, the one with the keyboards and the lack of customers. The place was naked, no pretty women or handsome men, just a few strangers, sitting brooding by the windows, dreaming of lovers who would someday stay. I joined one of them, and drank strong sugared coffee.

married, and she lives in Alabama now, with a family she's real proud of. She won't meet me, thinks it's better this way, and anyway I was very nearly aborted. I cry when I think of her, but I really don't know anything about her, we might hate each other, and besides, I cry all the time. Situations make me cry, and adults telling lies to their kids. They ought to cut the garbage, all the heaven and hell and persecution business. It's not only boring and moralistic, but it's sick. You grow up heartbroken and deceived, surrounded by assholes and apparent saviours. Nobody mentions class, or race, or unemployment, you think you can be a pilot or a ballet-dancer, and nobody will stop you. Enough of the hippie shit and the myths, the reality is mindblowingly different; you're probably ugly as sin, and will spend the whole of your life taking shit from others. Some get smart, rob or inherit, but I've done none of these, I'm just an expert in being fucked over.

I'd like to be wise, to see things coming, but it's not at all likely, unless it's my death; something I've rehearsed and perfected. Yes, when my hour of desperation tattoos itself upon my skin, I'll be more than

ready. Maybe I'll make thirty and mock my youth, but it's doubtful. It's not a James Dean thing, it's just I'm prone to accidents. You're worse; I've seen you, drinking yourself into comas, having your stomach pumped, for the sixth time (in a year). You love tragedy, you inject it so frequently, and your heroes, Janis and Jim, you'd probably smoke their ashes, if you could.

So winter's here, it's cold, and I'm in love with you. The leaves have shrivelled the last few weeks, and died leaving the trees naked, skinny, lonesome. Just looking at them I feel exposed, like somebody's ripped the clothes off my skin.

We're waiting for snow, only there's not been snow in nearly eight years. I'm curious to what it will feel like, falling softly against my face, but it's not arrived, not yet. No layers of crisp whiteness ready to be trampled on, no meticulous light or soft velvet. No angels wings, no nothing, only this same perishing air which absorbs us so easily. Chase the shadows out of those eyes, and keep dreaming of that girl you only ever meet in dreams. Imagine if you met, in an alleyway or a park, or even a shopping store, would it be too close to the bone?

I feel beat now. I walked the dog earlier, for what seemed like a forever. He hates the cold, and he refuses to run, until I'm worn out that is, and then he gets great surges of energy, whisking me off my feet. We walked, H.D and I, to the deli, for fresh bread and olives, but of course I ended up buying loads, avocado pears, feta cheese, and wine. The assistant was unhappy again, said her husband's having an affair, but she can't leave him, she's too scared of being alone. You know how I hate that, it's so weak. I mean, we all get lonely, but that's no reason to live with somebody, it's almost as pathetic as mercy fucking. You should be with someone because they make you feel good, or alive, or both. It's only by keeping fine company that you enjoy life, otherwise, well you're destined for destruction.

I keep looking at my photos of you and Bardot. You look so charming and so dizzy, a girl with problems and dilemmas. You look very young, like a homeless waif. It's strange, but when I look at these polaroids I think of my own childhood, and falling in lust and admiration with a woman my mother's age. She had grey hair and children, but she was with her girlfriend, and I gave her a single white rose, my knees shaking like the clappers. She thanked me, but I didn't understand, she spoke a different language, and I was too mesmerised to care. I left immediately afterwards, ran back to my table, and dreamt about being kissed by her, and her hands running over my fourteen year old body. I didn't sleep properly for a long time, and now? Now I'm far from innocent, in fact I could easily be a hustler or a pimp. I don't look to be saved, or even to be understood, only to not be broken.

How many chances do you think we get? I mean, at this love thing? The smell of incense drifts through the room, and I miss you, sweetly, tenderly, psychotically. Work was awful today, and I came home with such blues. I'm surrounded by fuckwits and jokers, whose conversation is reduced to simple banalities or cheap humour. At such moments, I wish I was mute, deaf, trapped in my own little world. I feel so damn restless, thinking about travelling, about doing something real. I would rather be offended or offensive, anything but this constant embrace of numbness. WHERE ARE 'OU? You with your exotic permes, your thousands of different ers, your mouth of rubies, your pping anorexic body, where? I ow there's a five o'clock train, d I desperately want to taste u, but I kind of dig this asochistic yearning, this endless issing you. How do you cope? u are alien to this world; sunine, rain, snow, thunder, nothing all disturbs you.

I ache for you, but I won't dmit it, not ever. I'll pretend u're out of my mind when we're t hanging out. Well, I know, it's a charmless lie, but for a girl that's apparently so cool and laid-back, aren't you a little too revealing? You say you miss me, you adore me, but I've watched you, able to flatter anyone or anything. Do you love me now, this very moment, or is the heat rising between you another? The girl before you, she was ALWAYS being unfaithful, enclosing others in her sultry rain, then lying through clenched shining teeth. 'Love you always and forever', don't ever tell me that one. I know sex outside of us doesn't mean you don't love me; lust is only natural. So, tell me, about your other loves? Last night I desired a redhead, a girl not more than nineteen, with a punk haircut and loose jeans. She was a great dancer, but her pupils were too starry, too sordid and bright; alive with the presence of moonbeams and ecstasy. You know what I'm talking about don't you, our sweet familiar friend cocaine, the friend that wraps you up so warm. The feeling, that is so delicious, so intimate, so comforting, especially the first few hits. I love screwing on coke, as you know, it makes me so alive,

each bone in my body rising to be touched
stroked, caressed, beaten. I didn't sleep with her though, didn't even flir
things were sweet enough. I called you instead, woke you for a little phon
sex.

I wanted to leave today, to pack my bags, check out of this god-damne
city. You could come with me, we'd pick up a few others, and merge ski
and bones to make a few bucks. I wouldn't mind watching you, an
besides, we need the cash to score with. You wouldn't let me get addicte
would you? I don't ever want to get addicted to anything, only th
lumination of the moon. The violet hours like these are m
favourite, the times that the heat really starts to rise, and you ca
do almost anything. The skyline was awesome tonight; pin
drooling over a sultry powder blue, with lavender dancing in th
background. Cities aren't so red in the winter-time, without th
glow of autumn, they seem blue, or navy, sometimes even black
What colour would you be? Denim probably, that very distinc
blue, which reflec
obsession, lonesomenes
and cruelty. Blue, th
colour that cuts itse
off

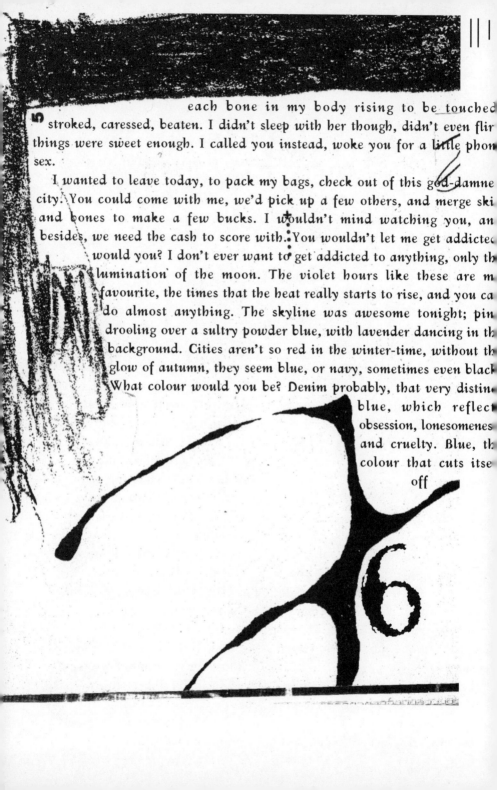

om everything. My ex was yellow, colour I craved and adored, but hen it arrived, I hated it. ideously bright, no subtlety or ftness, just an array of commer-al light. My colour? The colour of e seas, I guess, constantly chang-g, and polluted by outside forces. metimes I sparkle, but mainly I'm rely visible. You call me star, but n no such thing. Stars float from ch corner of the earth, they daz-e and enchant. Tonight there are ndreds, flickering and gleaming, aming us close together. If only u were here you'd see the beauty the silent skies, the craziness in is precise moment, and the nor-ality of it, passing by nearly eryone who lives here.

So what did you do tonight, when the electricity ran out? I bet you didn't snuggle up with your books of horror, did you? So much for being a lover of vam-pires, you wouldn't have dared tempt fate. What did you do then? Place those gentle hands upon your own silken thighs? Let your fin-gers dance where I wish I could? Was it good? I bet you thought of me, you couldn't have done it otherwise. You told me it was going to snow up there in that wild and rocky outback. Were you hoping that would get me on the next train? Well, it nearly did, but three days travelling is something I can't afford right now.

Shit I'm confused. Whatever I do, I feel your eyes burning into the back of my neck, opening up my sores and wounds, attempting to sting, then heal them. I play your favourite 45's, and contem-plate the fact, since Ruby left me, I don't feel whole. Why do you love me? I suppose it doesn't really matter, and until you get here, my folk singers keep me company. You keep threatening you'll move here, but do you really want all that settling down lark? Frankly babe, most of us have been run away FROM, not to.

8

Aside from that, you hate staying in, and if we even started to anywhere homely, I'm sure you'd make us move.

It's dark now, pitch black, dark you can't see your own hand. If you look through a telescope you can see your own dreams, stars dancing and shining, and trying to shape themselves around your face. The rain continues, hard and heavy, pouring solidly in sheets. It wakes me quickly, beating against the window, and I love it, it's like waiting for a train which will probably never arrive, and if it does, it'll have no fixed destination.

I take my time, pulling on a shirt and collecting the mail. A letter from you, and a letter from a friend in London. He says I should stop holding on, and holding back, just take anything I want in life. Is this a way to amuse, or to enlighten me, I don't have a clue. The coffee machine groans impatiently, waiting to be fed. Can't face a cigarette yet, so I stand by the window and watch the rain. Some girl is out there dancing amidst the raindrops. I remember one hazy evening last summer, lifting my face to the sky, the water falling like soft kisses. I danced with a girl between marble statues in a water park. The fountains were switched off, the water was freezing, and salty, and we took our clothes off, pretending we felt nothing for each other. Driving home was like saying good-bye to an old lover, but it wouldn't have been the same; staying until morning, and the cops arriving to take the junkies away.

Are you awake yet? I plan to do very little this savoury November morning. Maybe write to lovers and old friends who I've kept on hold whilst waiting for storms. The winds have been wonderful, but not strong enough, not Wizard of Oz like I'd hoped. So, my sweetest dearest hypocrite, were you here, would you hold me? Curl me up in those fine strong arms of yours? I dream of that, and of those vacant eyes. You hardly ever smile, except when you're drunk, but let's face it, this world isn't going to suddenly get better. Let me hold you, please, because I'm sure as hell useless otherwise. Don't say you love me again, just say you'll come and stay awhile.

There's no-one in the kitchen, so I warm up the stove, heat peanut soup with broccoli and cheese. It tastes real thick and spicy, just how you like your food. I hate this kitchen though, it's so dark and concrete, not like yours. Do you remember what I did to you in there? How I tied you so you couldn't move, then kissed you for hours. I imagine it now, and you kiss me back softly and sweetly. (My memory is obviously exhausted, for in reality you swallow me whole, your mouth drowning mine.)

I turn on the radio, and fumble with the reception. A news bulletin, more horror and more recession. I am mystified, not about that, but that neither of us know ANYTHING about the planet we are stuck on. I haven't a clue what happens outside this house, outside the thought of your velvet womb. I know you sit in your orange and blue bedroom, decorated with jelly snakes, and I know you're waiting for the post. Did I send anything? I can't remember. Your parcel of leaves

arrived yesterday, a the photos of you t ing desperately ha to look natural. didn't work, it's n you, all that smili stuff, you need yo hours of brooding a vitriol. Hang on, t broadcaster is mu bling something, son thing about snow Alabama, and gue what? It's coming way. I crouch do on the cold tiles, a light my first cigare of the day. It tas beautiful, fills lungs with mus smoke, and I admi my poster of Brigi Bardot. She smok too, but she has wonderful mout which I just was born with. Still, stretch my limbs an wait, for you and t snow to come to me

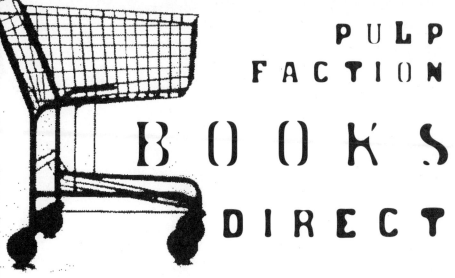

PULP FACTION BOOKS DIRECT

Order your copy of any Pulp Faction book direct,

and **save 25%** or more on the cover price

Please send me

1 book £4.50
2 books £8.00
3 books £11.00*

Skin   *no of copies*
Technopagan   *no of copies*
Homeland   *no of copies*

*Prices valid until 30 Sept 1995

next 3 issues (£11.00)

....*name*

....*address*

tick

....

....

....*postcode*

I enclose a cheque payable to the Pulp Faction

Charge my mastercard/ visa card, expiry date: ....

number: ....

Return to: Books Direct, Pulp Faction
60 Alexander Road, London N19 3PQ